"I didn't come all the way to Alaska to make foot lotion for the dogs, Ben. I want to work *with* the dogs."

"Paw ointment." He spat out the words. "And it's a very important part of the race."

"I'm sure it is." Her blond curls whipped around her face in the cold wind. Even in her angry, disheveled state, she still looked like a princess. "But I'm here as a sled dog handler."

"Clementine, it's not an easy job. You could get hurt." *And what if I can't save you?*

"At least I'll get hurt doing something amazing."

Ben's stomach tied itself in a familiar knot. "You don't know what you're saying."

She crossed her arms and lifted one brow.

Ben knew better than to think she'd changed her mind. Everything within him told him to keep walking. He couldn't protect Clementine. He couldn't even protect her silly dog. Experience had taught him that much, in the cruelest way possible.

But he was helpless to resist the strange pull he felt toward her.

TERI WILSON

grew up as an only child and could often be found with her head in a book, lost in a world of heroes, heroines and exotic places. As an adult, her love of books has led her to her dream career—writing. Now an award-winning author of inspirational romance, Teri spends as much time as she can seeing exotic places for herself, then coming home and writing about them, of course. When she isn't traveling or spending quality time with her laptop, she enjoys baking cupcakes, going to movies and hanging out with her family, friends and five dogs. Teri lives in San Antonio, Texas, and loves to hear from readers. She can be contacted via her website at www.teriwilson.net.

Alaskan Hearts

Teri Wilson

Love Inspired

Recycling programs
for this product may
not exist in your area.

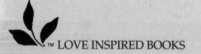

™ LOVE INSPIRED BOOKS

ISBN-13: 978-0-373-81629-3

ALASKAN HEARTS

www.LoveInspiredBooks.com

Printed in U.S.A.

I have come that they may have life,
and have it to the full.
—*John* 10:10

For Cameron.
I'm so proud of the young man you've become.

And to my husband, David, for giving me the
time and encouragement to pursue my dreams.

Acknowledgments

Many thanks to my special writing friend
Beckie Ugolini, for all the hours spent reading,
revising, cheering me on and having fun
over coffee. Also, thanks to my wonderful agent
Liz Winick for seeing the potential in my writing
and making the phone call that changed my career.
And thanks to Rachel Burkot, the most supportive
editor in the world! I feel so blessed to be part of the
Love Inspired family. And thank you to my critique
partners Tamra, Beckie, Sydney and Lupe.

This book is also dedicated to the people and dogs
of Alaska's Iditarod Trail Sled Dog Race.
I think I left a piece of my heart in Alaska the
first year I volunteered at the race. I'll see you again
next year and the year after that!

Chapter One

Clementine Phillips stared at the dead fish on the wall, only inches from her face, and shuddered. She'd shuddered quite a bit since arriving in Aurora, Alaska, but this time it wasn't a result of the subzero temperatures.

Her gaze shifted from the enormous fish to the brass nameplate hanging directly beneath it. *Wild Alaskan Salmon,* it read.

Clementine looked back at the salmon, scrunched her brow and tried to reconcile this monstrous creature with the contents of the frozen dinner she'd eaten while sitting in her cubicle at *Nature World* magazine not more than twelve hours ago. Lean Cuisine. Wild Alaskan salmon in basil sauce. An homage to finally embarking on the research assignment of a lifetime.

She and her officemate, Natalie, had eaten twin low-cal, instant meals and toasted Clementine's newfound freedom with diet sodas. Clementine hated to think about the fact that she'd landed this same assignment a year ago but turned it down to appease her worrywart fiancé.

Those days were over, as her ringless finger could attest to.

She forced the unpleasant memory from her mind and focused once again on the fish gaping at her.

Wild Alaskan salmon...just the name brought a smile to her lips. Every time she'd heard of Alaskan salmon, it was always preceded by the word *wild.* Was there even such a thing as tame Alaskan salmon? Or domesticated Alaskan salmon? It was always either wild Alaskan salmon or plain, generic salmon from nowhere.

Wild or not, she was surprised to discover salmon had such big teeth.

"How many photographs have I seen of grizzly bears snatching salmon out of raging rivers? Countless thousands," she murmured to herself. "And yet I never once knew they had teeth."

"Here you go," a grandfatherly voice boomed from behind her, followed by the thud of her luggage landing on the slippery floor of the hotel entrance.

Clementine searched the pocket of her parka for tip money, but soon realized one of her bags was missing from the pile. The most important bag of all. "Um, I don't see my..."

"Little pink bag?" The white-haired shuttle bus driver rolled his eyes and snorted. "Yeah, you're going to have to come get that one yourself. When I tried to pick it up, it growled at me."

Clementine's cheeks burned. She'd had every intention of dragging her own luggage inside, especially her dog carrier. But once she'd gotten a look at the ice-covered sidewalk, her confidence had wavered. Sidewalks in Texas weren't covered in ice. Not unless someone accidentally spilled a snow cone. Then again, the heat in Houston was often so unbearable that the ice would have melted before it hit the ground.

She pressed a few dollar bills into the driver's hand. "I'll be right out. Thank you."

"Sure thing," he grunted and clomped back to the shuttle bus. How he managed to clomp on three inches of ice, Clementine would never understand.

She shoved her suitcases against the wall, out of the way of the revolving doors she supposed led to the main lobby, and slipped into her parka. She pulled the zipper until it covered her entire mouth and the better part of her nose, heaved open the door and tiptoed onto the ice.

No sooner did her new pink UGGs make contact with the slick sidewalk than she slipped and went airborne. She squealed, closed her eyes and waited for the inevitable crash landing.

Except it never came. Instead, she found herself falling into a pair of very strong, masculine arms. Arms that belonged to an equally masculine voice.

"Whoa, there," the voice said, and Clementine

knew in an instant it wasn't the shuttle bus driver who had come to her rescue.

Her eyelids fluttered open and, with that first glance at the pair of glacial-blue eyes peering down at her with concern, the salmon flipped in her stomach. The one from the Lean Cuisine, not the wall.

Her rescuer smiled down at her, and his blue eyes crinkled in the corners in a most charming way. "Are you okay?"

Clementine swallowed. "Um, yes. A little rattled, that's all."

"Let me help you up." He lifted her to her feet, as if she weighed no more than her tiny Pomeranian, still waiting in the pink dog carrier in the shuttle bus.

"Thank you. I'm not accustomed to walking on ice." Her mind flashed briefly to the Bible story about Jesus walking on water. She supposed if the gospels had taken place in Alaska, he would have walked on ice. It would have been equally miraculous in Clementine's eyes.

"It comes with practice." The man glanced down at her new UGGs and frowned. The frown did nothing to lessen the effect of his startling blue eyes and deep dimples, visible even through his closely trimmed beard. "And shoes with better traction. Take very slow steps. That ought to help."

Something about the way he said it pricked Clementine's nerves. She had to stop herself from asking him what he could possibly know about women's shoes.

"Slow steps," she repeated curtly, with a nod. Clementine could do that. She was, in fact, an expert at taking slow steps. She'd been taking things slowly her entire life. Stepping on the plane to Aurora had been the most daring thing she'd ever done.

"This is your first trip to Alaska I take it?"

Clementine flushed, although whether from the realization that he still had a protective grasp on her arm or the fact that he seemed to read her thoughts, she wasn't sure. "Yes. Yes, it is."

"Enjoy your stay." He released her arm and lingered, watching to make sure she was steady on her feet.

"Thank you." She did her best to ignore his rugged good looks and instead focused on keeping her feet flat on the icy sidewalk. Not falling seemed like the best way to avoid a lecture on her choice of footwear. And she was having enough trouble maintaining her balance without thinking about those dimples. "And thank you again for the rescue."

"Anytime." He winked and headed toward the parking lot.

Clementine followed him with her gaze and couldn't help but notice his steps were most definitely not slow. In fact, they were downright brisk.

Then again, he looked Alaskan. He'd probably had more than enough practice walking on ice.

"Ahem." The gruff voice of the shuttle bus driver interrupted her thoughts. "Are you coming or do you need some help?"

"No, I've got it." She took a quick glance over her shoulder to check on her bags. They still sat right where she'd left them, under the cold, watchful eye of the mounted salmon.

Wild Alaskan salmon.

The words danced in her head.

Maybe *everything* in Alaska was wild. It certainly looked that way in the many photographs she'd sorted through for the magazine throughout the years. She thought about the calendar of Alaskan sled dogs that hung above her computer monitor. Mark had given it to her last year when she'd turned down the assignment in Alaska. As if looking at photos of Alaska could ever take the place of actually being there.

The dogs on her calendar looked nothing like her own sweet Pomeranian. They had hungry eyes and paws that moved so fast that they were nothing more than a blur.

Wild Alaskan sled dogs.

She laughed. She'd be willing to bet money they didn't even have cubicles in Alaska. Or Lean Cuisines.

And maybe, simply going to such a place could change a person. Take an ordinary girl with an ordinary life and transform her into someone just a little bit wild herself.

Clementine could only hope so.

She repeated the words from John 10:10 to herself, the words she'd clung to since finally making the break with Mark.

I have come that they may have life, and have it to the full.

A shiver ran up her spine. She looked around for the blue-eyed stranger who'd rescued her from falling, but he'd vanished in the darkness. Anticipation swelled in her chest, and she inhaled a deep breath as she took her first tentative step onto the ice.

Oh Lord, I hope so.

Ben Grayson paused in front of the revolving door of the Northern Lights Inn, half hoping to find the woman who had fallen into his arms earlier. The woman with the mass of blond curls spilling from the fur-lined hood of her parka and the less-than-appropriate footwear.

When he found himself alone in the bitter cold, he pushed the memory of her delicate features out of his mind and whistled for his Alaskan husky.

"Kodiak, come on."

The dog trotted to Ben's side and nudged his head square underneath the palm of his hand.

Kodiak had always been an expert nudger.

"Subtle." Ben gave him an affectionate scratch behind the ears.

The husky nuzzled against his knee until Ben pulled a worn, leather leash out of the pocket of his parka. As soon as Kodiak got a glimpse of the leash, his plumed tail uncurled into a straight line and hung between his hind legs. He furrowed his doggy brow and gazed up at Ben with sad copper eyes.

"Don't look at me like that. I'm not any happier about being here than you are, you know." He snapped the leash onto Kodiak's collar and told himself this was the last year he would darken the door of this place during race week. Even beautiful blonde women in need of rescue weren't enough to keep him coming back. The way he saw it, there was no reason he couldn't commute from his secluded cabin on the outskirts of Aurora to the official race events.

The plan was simple. Drive in, snap a few photos, drive out.

His boss at the *Yukon Reporter* didn't quite agree. He had all sorts of reasons why Ben needed to be "in the thick of things" at the race headquarters. That, and the very real threat of an avalanche wiping out the one highway between Knik and Aurora, kept him coming back year after year.

So here he was. Again.

But this was absolutely the last time he would agree to this arrangement. He breathed out a weary sigh and led Kodiak into the hotel lobby.

He stomped the snow from his boots and looked around for a clock. This was a wasted effort, as every available square inch of wall space played host to some sort of mounted animal head. There was the customary Alaskan moose hanging above the enormous stone fireplace, surrounded by a variety of antlered cousins. Above the coffee bar, a bison watched over the mixing of flavored lattes and cappuccinos. Next to the registration desk, the full body of a polar bear rose up on its back legs and towered over guests waiting to check in.

Ben groaned when he saw the crowd of people waiting in line. His heavy eyelids told him it had to be well past midnight, but from the look of things, half the population of the Lower Forty-Eight—as Alaskans called the rest of the United States—stood between him and a room key.

"Welcome to race week." A large hand smacked Ben between the shoulder blades. Hard enough that he dropped Kodiak's leash amid a sudden coughing fit.

"Sorry." Reggie Chase's dark face split into a wide grin. "I would have thought living out there in the middle of nowhere would have toughened you up by now."

"You live even farther out than I do," Ben managed to sputter as his ability to speak returned. "Remember?"

"Oh, yeah." Reggie wore mukluks, the traditional winter moccasins common to those living in the bush. For as long as Ben had known Reggie, he'd made his home in the remote village of Prospect. Reggie enjoyed living in the bush, away from the road network. "Off the grid," as he called it. Ben's cabin in the woods seemed cosmopolitan by comparison, even with its long-abandoned doghouses dotting the landscape.

Reggie let out a hearty laugh. "I saw your name tag over at the registration desk and wondered when you'd be rolling in. There's just one problem—that tag still says *Media* after your name."

Ben's jaw clenched, and a familiar throbbing flared in his temples. "Don't start."

"It's a shame to let that nice dog yard out at your place sit empty. That's all." Reggie crossed his arms, leaned closer and lowered his voice. Ben noticed his beard had grown a shade or two closer to silver since last year's Gold Rush Trail. "How many years has it been, friend?"

"You were the one who packed away all my sledding equipment, remember? You know exactly how many years it's been."

Four.

The number hung, unspoken, in the awkward space between them.

Four years, five...ten. Ben knew without a doubt the passing of time would in no way dim the memory of the land surrounding his cabin, once scattered with sledding equipment. A sled here, a cabled line there. After the accident that had ended his mushing career, Ben couldn't bring himself to touch any of it. He was afraid of his own muscle memory—that the drive bow would still feel comfortable in his hands. He'd let the snow cover it all, inch by inch, day by day, until it became nothing more than a series of mysterious white mounds. Then one day, he'd come home from work and they were gone. His yard was flat, smooth and white as a snow-covered sea of ice. Ben had been almost afraid to walk on it. He'd sat in his car and stared at his property—an unnatural blank slate—until darkness hovered on the horizon.

He'd found his equipment cleaned, polished and carefully stacked in the shed out back. Reggie's work to be sure, although he'd never admitted as much. Ben had taken one look, locked the door to the storage shed and never opened it again.

Now he massaged his forehead with his thumb and index finger. It made no difference. The throbbing only intensified. A war was being waged in his head, full of long-forgotten memories of the trail fighting to make themselves known. "Kodiak is the only dog I need these days."

Reggie's nostrils flared as he blew out a frustrated puff of breath. Let him be frustrated. Reggie could join the long list of people, led by Ben's very own father, who were all frustrated with him. Ben couldn't care less. "Where did that monster run off to anyway?"

At that precise moment, Kodiak's deep bark echoed off the wood-paneled walls, followed by a distinctly feminine squeal.

"That didn't sound good." Despite his ominous declaration, Reggie chuckled.

"Kodiak!" Ben called.

By now, the barking had grown louder. Ben followed the sound to the crowd of people waiting at the registration desk, in the shadow of the outstretched paws of the rampant polar bear.

The group parted like the Red Sea as he approached, revealing a woman with thick waves of blond hair standing alone, frozen to the spot.

Her. Ben's heart leaped with recognition.

Despite the way the color was draining from her face with alarming speed, she possessed a sort of innocent beauty. That, coupled with her mass of platinum curls, gave her the air and grace of a princess.

A princess who looked woefully out of place in Alaska.

Ben tore his gaze from her delicate face and took notice of the small pink suitcase at her feet, which for some reason rendered Kodiak spellbound.

The suitcase yipped. Kodiak yipped right back at it.

"Kodiak, no." Ben stepped forward and picked up the leash, which was dragging on the floor behind the husky.

The suitcase yipped again. Kodiak whined, craned his neck toward the mysterious bag and swept Ben's foot with his wagging tail.

With Kodiak safely restrained, the color returned to the woman's face in the form of a scarlet flush. It settled in the vicinity of her exquisite cheekbones.

"You." She scooped the pink bag off the floor and hugged it to her chest.

"I'm sorry if he frightened you." Ben ruffled the

fur on the scruff of Kodiak's neck. "He wouldn't hurt a fly. He just likes to make noise."

"I'm not scared."

Clearly a bald-faced lie. She couldn't have looked more terrified if the stuffed polar bear suddenly sprang to life and romped around the lobby. "All the same, I apologize."

"Apology accepted." Her reddened cheeks faded to a soft pink, the exact shade of her barking bag. And her fuzzy sweater. And those ridiculous shoes, which resembled some sort of sheepskin bedroom slippers. If sheep were pink.

Ben pointed to the bag. "What have you got in there? Whatever it is, my dog finds it fascinating."

She smiled and gave the bag a little squeeze. "This is Nugget."

He glanced down at Kodiak, who had flattened himself to the ground and was attempting a commando crawl to get to the bag. "Nugget, as in a tasty morsel for Alaskan huskies?"

Her lips settled into a straight line. "Nugget, as in my dog's name."

"I was only joking." Ben gave Kodiak's leash a tug to put some more distance between him and Nugget. "Although you might want to be careful. To some of the dogs around here, that purse will look an awful lot like a lunch box."

"It's not a purse," she deadpanned. "It's a dog carrier."

Ben resisted the urge to laugh, figuring it would

only lead to another apology. Purse, dog carrier…
what was the difference? What kind of dog would
actually fit into something that small? Kodiak would
have outgrown that thing by the time he was twelve
weeks old. "Dog carrier. Got it."

His response seemed to satisfy her, if the return
of her sweet smile was any indication. "Can I ask
you a question?"

Weariness had begun to settle in his bones and
the line at the registration desk had at last thinned
out, but Ben found himself agreeing. "Sure."

She slipped the *dog carrier* over her shoulder.
Ben could see two tiny eyes staring at him through
a mesh panel on the side of the bag. "Are they all
this loud? Wild Alaskan huskies?"

The way her green eyes widened when she said
it brought a smile to Ben's lips—a genuine smile.
It had been a long time since he'd smiled like
that. It felt strange. "They're just Alaskan huskies.
You can drop the *wild*."

She bit her full lip. "Of course. I knew that."

"And the answer is no." Ben looked down at
Kodiak, who'd finally given up on his quest to meet
the elusive Nugget. The bigger dog had rolled onto
his back, with his tongue lolling out of the side of
his mouth.

"Really?"

He wasn't sure why it made him glad to see that
she looked more curious than relieved. "Most of
them are louder."

She laughed. "I've seen them in photographs so many times. I just didn't realize."

"They tend to be quieter on film." *I ought to know,* he thought.

"I want to be prepared." Her smile grew wider and her eyes sparkled like a kid on Christmas morning.

"Are you staying for the race?" She had to be. Why else would she be here, now of all times? Although he couldn't imagine, for the life of him, why a woman like her would have any interest in the Gold Rush Trail sled-dog race.

"Of course. That's what brought me here, to Alaska." The sparkle in her eyes intensified when the word *Alaska* passed her lips.

A tangle of dread formed in the pit of Ben's stomach. She wasn't saying…no, she couldn't be.

As if she could read his mind, she filled in the blanks for him. "I'm here to work with the dogs."

Ben narrowed his gaze at her. "In what capacity, exactly?"

"I'm going to be a sled dog handler!" There was no way to describe her enthusiasm other than to say she was actually gushing.

Ben couldn't help it. His mouth dropped open in shock. Did she have any idea what she was saying?

"Next!" a voice bellowed from the front desk.

"That's us." The woman—Ben still didn't even know her name—gazed lovingly down at the pink dog carrier and hitched it farther up on her shoulder.

She wiggled her fingers in a wave. "'Bye, Kodiak. 'Bye, Kodiak's Dad."

As she turned to head for the registration desk, Ben caught a glimpse of Nugget watching him from behind the mesh screen. Just as he suspected, the tiny creature in no way resembled a real dog.

Sled dog handler?

She couldn't possibly be serious.

Chapter Two

Clementine wiggled her toes in the comfy warmth of her UGGs and looked out the window at the blinding swirl of white.

Snow.

It was everywhere. Piled up waist-deep along the carefully shoveled streets and the labyrinth of narrow sidewalks surrounding the hotel. And to Clementine's complete and utter delight, it was still coming down in buckets.

Buckets...that might be more of a rain-related expression.

She struggled for an appropriate metaphor as she scooped Nugget into her arms. "Look, Nugget, it's snowing cats and dogs."

She supposed that didn't really work, either. But it was the best she could do, because she'd never actually seen snow before. Other than in photographs anyway.

Of course it had been snowing last night when she

and her queasy stomach finally escaped the airplane and caught the shuttle bus to the Northern Lights Inn. She hadn't been able to fully appreciate the beauty of an Alaskan snowfall at such a late hour. This morning was a different story, however. She'd never seen anything like it. The coastal Texas area wasn't exactly known for its harsh winter weather. It had snowed only once in Houston during Clementine's lifetime. She had been four years old, too young to carry any memory of making a snowman in her front yard into her adult life. She'd seen the photos, though, in the thick albums that filled her parents' bookshelves. The snowman had been a full head taller than she was. But, like so many things in Clementine's life, she knew the experience only through pictures.

Not anymore.

She looked out on the strange, white world and was struck by the purity of it all.

Though your sins are like scarlet, they shall be white as snow.

She would never think of those holy words the same way again.

Thank You, Lord, for Your love and forgiveness. And thank You for bringing me here. At last.

Tears pricked the corners of her eyes, but she sniffed and blinked them back. She scooped Nugget into her arms. "How would you like to go for our first walk in the snow?"

The hotel lobby was even busier than the night before and, save for the numerous dead animals on the walls, it seemed everyone had an official Gold Rush Trail name tag hanging around their neck. Clementine almost felt naked without one. A huge banner that read "Welcome Gold Rush Trail Volunteers!" was hoisted above a smooth, lacquered counter at the foot of the staircase. Behind the counter, a map of Alaska covered the wall, floor-to-ceiling. The trail the sled dog teams would cover during the race was marked out in red dashes, all the way from Aurora to the village of Nome, close to the Arctic Circle.

Look at that! I'm almost at the top of the world!

"Can I help you?" A tall woman wearing a neon-orange skullcap greeted her from behind the desk.

"Oh, sure." Clementine took a step closer to the counter, and Nugget followed along at the end of her pink leather leash.

"Cute dog." The woman, whose name was Bea, according to her name tag, smiled down at the Pomeranian. "We're all dog lovers around here, although we don't often see ones that are so tiny."

Clementine's thoughts immediately turned to the handsome man she'd met the night before—Kodiak's dad. He was so rugged, so *Alaskan*. She remembered with less fondness his warning about Nugget looking more like a snack than a canine. And his reprimand about her shoes. "I'll keep a close eye on her."

"Good idea." Bea nodded. "Are you a volunteer? Can I help get you checked in?"

"Yes. My name is Clementine Phillips from Houston, Texas. I'm a researcher for *Nature World* magazine. They sent me to volunteer and report back about the race."

Bea flipped through the box of name badges on the countertop until she found the right one. "So you're volunteering as a…sled dog handler?"

Her gaze flitted to Nugget once again, and her lips twitched into a smirk.

Clementine tightened her grip on Nugget's leash. "Yes."

"Have you ever worked with sled dogs before?" Bea appeared to be putting forth great effort to not look directly at Nugget anymore.

"Um, not exactly." Did sifting through photos of sled dogs for *Nature World* count? She certainly wasn't going to mention that she'd never actually seen one in the flesh—er, fur—until last night. "But there's a training class, right?"

"Yes." Bea's voice turned dead serious. "The class is mandatory if you don't already have your sled dog handler certification card."

"I'll be there. I've already registered for the class."

"Good. It's *mandatory*."

"I understand." What was her problem?

"Even if you have a Ph.D. in dog, you've got to take the class." She held out Clementine's name tag but didn't appear willing to let it go.

Clementine tugged on it a few times until she finally managed to wrestle it out of Bea's reluctant fingers. *Good grief!* "Thanks again for the reminder. I'll be at the class. It's tomorrow afternoon, right?"

"Tomorrow at noon." She glanced down at Clementine's pink UGGs. "Dress warm. You'll be spending an hour or two outside in the parking lot."

Clementine resisted the urge to salute and say "Yes, ma'am." She said a silent prayer of thanks for Bea's neon hat. At least she would be able to see her coming from a distance, and she could run in the other direction. "Okay."

"Here's your volunteer hat and T-shirt." She slid them across the counter with no small amount of reluctance.

Clementine took the items and slipped her lanyard over her head, with her name tag facing outward. *There!* She looked as official as all of the other people milling about. "Thank you."

"You know..." Bea called out to her as she turned to go. "You can always change your mind. We have plenty of other volunteer jobs. Like filing. Or answering phones."

Clementine's face burned, and it was a struggle to keep her voice even. "No, thank you. I'm here to work with the dogs."

Honestly. Filing? Answering telephones? Those wouldn't exactly make fascinating topics for an article in the magazine. She might as well be sitting back in her cubicle in Texas.

Even as the thought crossed her mind, her cell

phone vibrated in her pocket. She pulled it out and examined the screen.

Sure enough, her cubicle had managed to follow her to Alaska.

She cleared her throat, just in case it was her boss. If she didn't come off as confident, he'd never send her anywhere again. He most certainly didn't need to know the race personnel were trying to talk her into answering phones. "Hello?"

"Clementine, thank goodness. You made it in one piece." Natalie Marshall, her officemate, sighed into the phone.

Clementine's heart lifted at the sound of her voice. In addition to sharing a cubicle, she and Natalie were good friends. As close as two people who spend forty-plus hours a week within five feet of one another could be.

She settled on one of the brown leather sofas in the lobby and scooped Nugget into her lap. "I'm here."

"Are you frozen solid?"

Clementine laughed. "Almost."

"You asked for it. Remember? Over and over and over again, as I recall."

"Oh, I recall." Clementine's voice turned wistful as she thought about all the times she'd begged to go on one of the plum research assignments out in the field, and the grim look on her fiancé's face last year when she told him she'd finally gotten the one in Alaska.

It hadn't been the first sign of trouble in their engagement, but it had been the one that really got her attention. Then, six short months later, there was no engagement.

Natalie whispered into the phone, signaling her call wasn't all about work. "Listen, you will not believe what I saw driving down Memorial Drive this morning."

Clementine took a wild guess. "A car?"

"No. I mean there were cars, obviously, but that's not what I'm talking about," Natalie huffed.

Clementine could almost hear her eyes roll from a thousand miles away. "What did you see driving down the street that was so interesting?"

"A motorcycle, complete with red flames on the side. I think it might have been a Harley. And guess who was riding it?" She didn't wait for Clementine to speculate. It was a good thing because in a million years she never would have guessed the identity of the bike's rider. "Mark!"

"Mark?" Clementine paused, trying to absorb this information. The pause served no purpose, however. She would never be able to wrap her mind around Mark on a Harley. Unless Harleys suddenly came in beige. "As in my ex-fiancé, Mark?"

"The one and only."

Impossible.

Mark didn't believe in motorcycles. Or any other type of vehicles with flames. Mark was safe. He wanted to live his life in a harmless little box.

He'd certainly wanted to keep Clementine in a box.

"What a hypocrite." Natalie's voice rose above a whisper with this proclamation. "Can you believe him?"

"Mark doesn't concern me anymore." Even faced with the literally *flaming* evidence of his double standard, she honestly meant it. She felt nothing at the mention of his name. A fact that spoke volumes.

Although a part of her couldn't help but wonder if he'd been right about Alaska. The attitudes of the people she'd met so far weren't exactly encouraging.

Clementine gulped. "I'm in Alaska and I'm about to go enjoy my first snowfall."

"Good for you. Forget about all of us back home, Mark included, and enjoy your trip. This is the adventure you've been waiting for." Clementine could hear the hum of a computer monitor in the background and the familiar clickety-clack of Natalie's fingers flying over the keyboard. "I've got to run. Duty calls. You take care."

The line went dead. Clementine stared at the darkened screen and made a mental note to make sure to buy Natalie a souvenir before she went home. Something nice. A little piece of Alaska. She deserved it for holding down the fort in their cubicle while Clementine was off on her adventure.

She shoved the phone back in her pocket and headed toward the revolving door, anxious to get outside and sink her feet into the snow. Before she pushed her way through, she paused and pulled four tiny shoes from the other pocket of her parka. Correction—*booties,* not shoes. That's what they called them here in Alaska. All the sled dogs wore them, and even dogs who weren't professional athletes. They protected canine feet from the hazards of exposure to ice and snow.

It just happened to be an added bonus that the ones she'd found online for Nugget were beyond adorable.

She taped them into place. The little Pomeranian was remarkably cooperative, considering she'd never actually been a shoe-wearing dog before.

Bootie-wearing, not shoe-wearing.

With the booties firmly fastened, Clementine stood and admired them. Nugget pranced for a few steps and spun in a quick circle.

"Good girl," Clementine cooed.

This was going so well that she'd have to consider the possibility of using them back home. Surely somewhere in Texas there existed a logical reason for a dog to wear booties. She'd lived there her entire life and never stumbled across such a reason, but that didn't mean one didn't exist. Right?

"It looks like we're ready to brave the cold. Let's go, Nugget." She headed outside with a booty-clad Nugget bobbing at the end of her leash.

The revolving door had barely spun them out on the snowy pavement when a blast of frigid air hit Clementine in the face. It was cold. Biting cold. Arctic cold. Colder-than-her-parents'-fancy-subzero-refrigerator cold.

Despite the burning sensation in her lungs when she inhaled, Clementine smiled into the wind. This was her first day in Alaska, her first snow-covered morning since that long-forgotten day chronicled in her family photo albums. And she knew exactly how she was going to spend it.

Ben snapped the lens cap on his camera and slid it into his shoulder bag. His fingers ached from the cold, and as soon as the camera was put away, he stuffed his hands back into his pockets for the comfort of the hand-warmer packets he always kept inside. *Comfort* might have been a stretch, but they helped a little. As much as he could expect anyway.

Reggie walked silently beside him, his dark eyes tracing Ben's every move. Between them, Kodiak moved in a relaxed lope. He panted softly, his breath coming out in soft clouds with each step.

"Your hands still giving you trouble?" Reggie raised his brows.

Ben shrugged. "Sometimes. Nothing I can't handle." He knew Reggie had noticed. His keen eyes didn't miss much, an attribute that made him a fine dog musher.

Reggie shook his head. "You need some mittens. Good ones. Beaver or moose hide."

Ben laughed to himself. Good old Reggie. If he couldn't turn Ben into a musher again, he would at least make sure he looked like one. "I've still got my old ones, but it's a little hard to take photographs with my fingers encased in moose hide."

"You and your pictures." An eye roll followed. "You make sure and keep those hand-warmer people in business. It's hard to booty a dog without any fingers."

Ben didn't bother reminding Reggie there would be no dog-bootying in his future. It was a waste of breath. His energy was better spent trying to change the subject altogether. "Thanks for letting me get some shots of your dogs this morning. I think we got a few good ones."

"No problem." Reggie's dark face creased into a grin. The pride he felt in his team showed clearly in his expression. "Although you'd probably get more money for those pictures if they were of Mackey's dogs."

"Every other photographer here is taking photos of Mackey's dogs." Ben squinted into the distance. He could see clear across the parking lot to where the throng of photographers clustered around the three-time champion's truck with its musher box on top. "No, thanks."

Mackey was the musher to beat, the sport's greatest champion. Once upon a time, Ben had been the musher to beat.

He pushed the thought away and concentrated instead on the comfort of the hand warmers.

"You might want to get that camera out again,

friend. Here's something else your competition is missing out on." Reggie slowed to a stop.

Ben turned away from the Mackey hoopla and followed the direction of Reggie's gaze toward a snowy embankment off to the side of the hotel. The area was deserted, save for a lone woman, with a tiny creature yapping and dancing around her feet. Ben knew in an instant it was the same woman from last night—the one who referred to him as "Kodiak's dad." The tiny ball of fur beside her must be Nugget, even though Nugget resembled a squirrel more than any dog Ben had ever seen. A lopsided tower of snow was heaped next to them and looked as though it might topple over at any moment.

Ben resisted the nonsensical urge to run over, sweep her out of the way and into his arms. He cleared his throat. "Would you look at that?"

"Pink booties." Reggie shielded the sun from his eyes with his hands, probably to get a better look. "She's got pink booties on that dog."

Ben pulled his camera from his bag and looked through the telephoto lens. He told himself it was only to verify that Nugget was in fact a member of the canine species. "They've got ears."

"Of course they have ears. Although if she doesn't cover hers with a hat, she might just lose 'em. Like you and your fingers." Reggie laughed aloud at his own joke.

"Not the woman…the booties." Ben handed Reggie his camera. Someone else had to get a look at this. "This doesn't make a bit of sense, but I think they might be bunny slippers."

"What? Bunny slippers?" Reggie furrowed his brows and peered through the camera. He shook his head and handed it back to Ben. "Well, I'll be. What do you suppose she's doing out there anyway?"

Ben watched her grab an armful of snow with her bare hands and add it to the heap. Her cheeks and nose glowed bright pink from the cold, which didn't seem to bother her in the slightest. She bounced around her snowy creation and scrutinized it from all angles.

A slow smile found its way to Ben's lips. "I think she's making a snowman."

Reggie snorted with laughter. "Cheechako. It figures."

Irritation pricked Ben's nerves. He couldn't say why. He'd used the same word to describe newcomers to Alaska countless times. Everyone did. There wasn't anything inherently disrespectful about it.

Still, he wasn't laughing. "You go on ahead. I'm going to get a few shots of the dog."

"That dog?" Reggie nodded his head toward Nugget. "Seriously?"

Ben shrugged and looked through the viewfinder again. "You never know, my editor might use it as a human interest–type piece."

"I can see it now. My sled dogs are going to get upstaged by a puffball that wears bunny slippers."

Reggie shook his head and wandered toward the hotel. "I'm off to the mushers' meeting."

"Later," Ben muttered, entranced by the sight of the woman through his zoom lens. There was something about the way she seemed to glow from the inside out…he found it fascinating.

What am I doing? I'm supposed to be getting shots of the dog, not acting like some sort of stalker.

He redirected his lens to the little dog, who was busy kicking up a fine dust of snow with her pink booties. It didn't take long to get a dozen or so shots, the majority of which were guaranteed to make the most hardened sourdough crack a smile. Even one like Reggie.

Just to be on the safe side, he snapped a few more. Kodiak waited by his side, with his paw resting on the top of Ben's left foot, until the camera was packed away again.

Ben patted Kodiak between his pricked ears. "Let's go say hello and let her know I took some photos."

If only to assure himself he was a journalist, and most definitely *not* a stalker, he needed to get permission to use the pictures. He snapped Kodiak's leash in place and headed over to the trio—woman, dog and snowman.

The closer they got, the more excited Kodiak became, until he let out a prolonged *woo-woo*. Nugget responded by pawing frantically at her owner's shins.

"Good morning, Kodiak's Dad." She scooped the little pup into her arms and directed her blinding smile at Ben.

A smile so bright that it almost hurt his eyes to look directly at it. "Hey, there, Nugget's Mom."

"It's Clementine, actually." Ben wouldn't have thought it was possible for her smile to grow wider, but it did.

"Nice to meet you, officially. I'm Ben." He glanced at the name tag dangling from the lanyard around her neck. Sure enough, it indicated her name was Clementine Phillips, from Houston, Texas. *Texas.* That explained her unabashed glee at the freshly fallen snow. "Something tells me this is the first time you've seen so much snow."

She laughed and cast a sheepish glance toward the lopsided snowman. "How could you tell?"

Ben followed her gaze and took in Frosty's egg-shaped head and his drooping stick arms. "Lucky guess."

"My first snowman, too. Well, sort of." Nugget wiggled in her arms and craned her tiny head toward Kodiak. Clementine looked at Ben, with questions shining her eyes. "Can I let her down? I think she wants to play."

"Sure." Ben unsnapped Kodiak's leash and ruffled the fur behind his ears. "Try not to step on your new friend, okay, buddy?"

Nugget barked and took off running, a sure invitation for Kodiak to chase her. The two dogs cut a path through the snow and made a big loop around Ben, Clementine and the snowman.

Ben nodded toward the dogs. "Nice bunny slippers, by the way. I took a few pictures of Nugget. I hope that's all right."

"Thank you." Clementine glanced at his name tag. "Media? Are you a reporter?"

"Photographer. For the *Yukon Reporter*." He averted his gaze away from Kodiak. He was a photographer now. That's all. No matter how fervently Reggie, along with the other mushers, tried to tell him otherwise.

Clementine simply smiled. For all she knew, he'd always been a photographer. It was a welcome relief. "You work for a paper? Really? I work as a media researcher back in Texas."

"Is that right? For a newspaper?"

"No." She shook her head and looked down at her feet, clad in the same pink sheepskin boots she'd worn the night before. This woman clearly had a thing for slippers. *"Nature World."*

"Nature World. That's impress…" Before Ben could finish his thought, he caught a glimpse of movement out of the corner of his eye. He snapped his head to the right, just in time to see Nugget and Kodiak barrel into the side of Clementine's snowman.

Snow flew in every direction, but somehow the majority of it landed on Clementine's face. At first, she stood completely still. She seemed too shocked to do or say anything. Then, just as Ben reached to brush some of the snow away, she started giggling.

Soon she was laughing so hard that she could barely stand up straight. Kodiak joined in, barking at the top of his lungs, until he resumed digging at a pile of snow in search of a halfway-buried Nugget.

"Are you okay?" Ben wiped a wet blob of slush from her cheek. The cold water stung his thumb, but not so much that he failed to appreciate the softness of her skin.

Her cheeks flushed pinker than ever. "I'm fine. I'm a mess, but I'm fine." She wiped her laminated name tag against her parka to dry it off.

It was then that Ben noticed the words printed beneath her name and hometown. *Sled Dog Handler.*

He stiffened. He'd nearly forgotten why she was here. "So you're still planning on handling dogs for the race?"

"Of course. The magazine sent me here for that explicit purpose." The giggling abruptly stopped. He thought he spotted a flicker of worry in her bright green eyes, but it vanished in an instant. "You thought I'd changed my mind since last night?"

Ben made a feeble attempt at a nonchalant shrug. "There are other things you can do, you know. I could probably get you involved with the group that's getting together to make the ointment for the dogs' paws."

"Why does everyone keep saying things like

that?" She threw her hands up in the air. Snow flew off a few of her fingertips.

"Well, you…"

She refused to let him finish. "I didn't come all the way to Alaska to make foot lotion. I want to work with the dogs."

"Paw ointment," he spat. "And it's a very important part of the race."

"I'm sure it is." She jammed her hands on her hips. Her blond curls whipped around her face in the cold wind. Even in her angry, disheveled state, she still looked like a princess. "But I'm here as a sled dog handler. I know I can do it."

Ben wasn't sure who she was trying to convince—him or herself.

"Clementine, it's not an easy job. You could get hurt." *And what if I can't save you?* The thought hit him like a cold slap in the face.

"So what if I do? At least I'll get hurt doing something with myself. Something amazing." Stars twinkled in her eyes. Naive, dangerous stars.

Ben's stomach tied itself in a familiar knot. "You don't know what you're saying."

"I'm pretty sure I'm saying that I'm going to handle sled dogs." She crossed her arms and lifted one perfect brow.

Ben clenched and unclenched his fists. He could barely feel his fingers anymore. The numbness was a reminder of everything he wished he could forget. "Fine, go ahead. Get yourself trampled. Or run over by a sled. That would be a lot more fun than making paw ointment, wouldn't it?"

He let out a sharp whistle and, when he was certain Kodiak was bounding toward him, he turned on his heel to walk away.

"Oh, Ben, guess what else I've never done before?" Behind him, Clementine's voice rang like a bell. Innocent, sweet.

Still, he knew better than to think she'd changed her mind.

Everything within him told him to keep walking. He couldn't protect Clementine. He couldn't even protect her silly dog. Experience had taught him that much, in the cruelest way possible.

But he was helpless to resist the strange pull he felt toward her.

Against his better judgment, he turned around. He barely had time to notice the snowball whizzing toward him before it hit him square in the forehead.

Chapter Three

Clementine watched in horror as the snowball flew toward Ben. With a squishy-sounding *splat,* it made contact with his forehead. His eyes widened as a blob of slush ran down his face and lodged in his closely trimmed beard.

Clementine was mortified to her very core.

Dear Lord, what has gotten into me?

She blamed it on Alaska. She'd gone wild. Just like the salmon.

"Your first snowball, I take it?" Ben wiped the slush from his beard and leveled his gaze at her.

"I was aiming at your back." She held up her hands in a gesture of surrender. "I promise."

"Unbelievable." He shook his head and one corner of his mouth tugged up into a crooked grin.

It was only half a smile, but she'd take what she could get. At the sight of it, Clementine released a relieved lungful of air. She stopped breathing again when he bent down and scooped a generous blob of snow into his big hands.

"I can't remember the last time I was part of a snowball fight." The gleam in his eyes was positively wicked as he went to work packing the snow into a perfect, round ball.

Clementine looked at the snowball with envy. *Wow, he's good.*

"Fortunately, it's like riding a bike. Some skills seem to stick with you." He came toward her and launched the snowball in one swift movement.

She squealed and ran toward the makeshift shelter of the pitiful remains of her snowman, but not before Ben's snowball hit the back of her parka with a thud.

"Wait!" she wailed, as she plunged her hands in the snow.

Ben pelted her with three more snowballs in rapid succession before she could even form one of her own. She wasn't sure if hers even qualified as a snowball. It wasn't quite round, if truth be told. It was shaped more like an amoeba.

She threw it as hard as she could and jumped up and down in delight when she discovered that snow amoebas were every bit as effective as snowballs. Ben's beard was once again covered in snow. He looked like Santa Claus.

Wild Alaskan Santa.

Laughter bubbled up Clementine's throat until tears streamed down her cheeks. She scrambled to form another snowball, but lost her balance on the slippery ground. She screamed through her laughter, even as Ben loomed over her with another of his perfectly packed snowballs.

He aimed it directly at her face and held it there, taunting her. "What's so funny?"

A cold drop of snow landed on her nose, and she let out a shriek. "Your beard is full of snow. You look like a certain man who dresses in red suits and has a fondness for caribou."

"Caribou, huh?" He lifted his brows. "You're starting to sound like a real Alaskan."

Her stomach flipped. "Really?"

His only response was to grind the snowball on the top of her head.

Ice-cold water ran down her curls, soaking her neck. A shiver ran up her spine. "I give up. You win."

He flashed a triumphant grin and Clementine shivered again, this time at the reappearance of those charming crinkles in the corners of his eyes. "Great. I suppose that means you'll reconsider the paw ointment idea."

And just like that, the crinkles lost their appeal.

"It means nothing of the sort," she spat. "You've won the battle, but not the war."

His grin faded, along with the laugh lines. "I don't want to be at war with you, Clementine."

The genuine concern written all over his face nearly did her in. "It's only an expression. We're not at war."

"Good." He offered his hand to help her up.

She took it and tried not to think about how comforting his grasp was. Or about how delicate and feminine she felt standing next to him. Those were dangerous thoughts. The sort of thoughts that would keep her from her destiny. Although sometimes she wondered what exactly that destiny might be. "Thank you."

"You're welcome." He peeled a few of her wet ringlets away from her face. "You're soaked. You should probably get inside."

Again with the unsolicited advice. Just like Mark. Two could play at that game. "And your hands are freezing. You should do the same."

Ben jammed his hands into his pockets and nodded his head toward the hotel. "Would you like to get some coffee? They usually have a daily special. I think today it's something called a toasted marshmallow latte."

Even the lattes here sounded exotic. Her mouth watered. "That sounds great, but..."

"But?" He swallowed, and his Adam's apple bobbed up and down in his throat.

She swept Nugget into her arms and narrowed her gaze at Ben. "You have to promise not to mention the foot lotion again."

His jaw visibly clenched. "You mean paw ointment?"

Nugget trembled against her chest. As much as she hated to admit it, Ben was right—she needed to get inside. She hoped that was all he was right about. "You know what I mean."

"Fine, I'll drop it." He released a sigh and picked up his camera bag from where it had fallen in the snow during their snowball fight. "For now."

As Ben led her to the coffee bar with his hand on the small of her back, Clementine tried not to think about how long it had been since she'd been on a date. There hadn't been anyone since Mark. Not that this qualified as a date. As inexperienced as she was in the rules of engagement for snowball fights, she supposed this could simply be some sort of truce ritual.

And to be honest, she wasn't sure if she wanted it to count as a date. Dating didn't really fit into the adventurous lifestyle she had in mind. Ben was certainly attractive. And so masculine. Nothing at all like the men back home. Beige would be the last word she would ever use to describe him.

He also thought she should spend her time making paw ointment instead of doing what she came here to do.

Let it go. He promised not to mention it again.

"What happened to you two?" The barista slid a single menu across the counter. "You look like a couple of drowned rats. Did you fall in the lake out back?"

"The lake is frozen solid, remember?" Ben nodded toward the big picture window behind the coffee bar. Behind the glass, what Clementine supposed was the lake stretched out like a blank, white canvas.

"That's right. This is Alaska. I almost forgot, seeing as you look like you just went for a swim." She cast a suggestive look in Clementine's direction.

Okay, so maybe this is a date.

She waited for the inevitable feeling of suffocation to set in, like it had every time she even considered dating since breaking things off with Mark.

But the feeling never came.

Instead, she was surprised to find herself overcome by a strange sensation. She glanced over at Ben, sitting beside her. He smiled and she felt light as a feather. She wondered if she might float right off the bar stool and bump heads with the enormous bison looking down on them.

Ben leaned closer. He smelled of spruce and freshly fallen snow, like Alaska itself. "So two toasted marshmallow lattes?"

Clementine opened her mouth and started to order hers skinny, like she always ordered her coffee from the coffee bar down the block from the *Nature World* offices. The barista raised her brows and waited for an answer. Behind her, Clementine could see a small airplane skidding to a landing on two skis smack in the middle of the frozen lake. She'd never seen a plane with skis before. She didn't even know such a thing existed. Probably because, like her coffee, everything in her life was boring. No fat, no whip, no sugar.

No life.

She tore her gaze from the plane with the skis and turned to Ben. "That sounds lovely. Can I have mine with extra whipped cream?"

"Of course." He handed the menu back to the barista. Clementine finally focused on her Northern Lights name badge long enough to notice that her name was Anya. "Two toasted marshmallow lattes. Extra whipped cream on both."

Anya scribbled a few lines on a notepad. "Coming right up. And I'll bring a bowl of water for the dogs."

Kodiak and Nugget lay curled together in the corner, under the belly of a stuffed grizzly bear standing on all fours. Clementine tilted her head and examined the fierce scowl on the bear's face. "You know, I've always thought Pomeranians looked sort of like bears, until now. Nugget doesn't look at all like that creature."

Ben laughed. "A teddy bear maybe. But she's no grizzly."

"Have you ever seen one?" She focused on the bear's huge, yellow teeth and gulped. "A live one, I mean?"

"A grizzly?" He shrugged, as if seeing a grizzly bear sauntering down one of Aurora's sidewalks would be no big deal.

Clementine nodded and forced herself to look away from the bear's snarl.

"Sure." Ben took the two fresh lattes from Anya and set one down in front of Clementine. He blew on his, creating a subtle dip in the mountain of whipped cream. "In the summertime, you can see them catching salmon right on the riverbank. That's why most everyone here carries bear insurance."

Clementine wrapped her hands around her cup of coffee to warm them, and considered Ben's comment. "Bear insurance? I don't think we have coverage for that in Texas."

He winked at her. "It's only an expression."

"For?"

He looked at her over the rim of his coffee cup, and his blue eyes turned serious. "Guns."

"Oh." She gripped her cup tighter.

"No one likes to shoot a bear, or any other creature for that matter. And ninety-nine percent of the time, it's not necessary. But this is Alaska. Things are different here. This can be a dangerous place and it never hurts to be prepared." His voice was gentle but firm.

Clementine's eyes widened and she whispered, "Are you telling me I need to get a gun?"

Ben choked on his latte with such force that he popped right off his bar stool. His face turned three shades of red.

"You okay, sport?" Anya asked. Without waiting for an answer, she pushed a glass of water toward him.

He sipped the water and waited until his color returned to a somewhat normal shade before he said anything. Then, finally, he sat down again and spoke

through clenched teeth. "I am most definitely *not*
telling you to go out and get a gun. In fact, I forbid
you to do any such thing."

"*Forbid* me? Ha!" Clementine slung back a gulp
of her coffee. The moment it touched her tongue,
she decided that fat lattes were infinitely superior
to skinny lattes. "You can't tell me what to do, Ben
Grayson. You don't even know me. You, you…lotion
peddler."

"For the last time, it's *paw ointment*." He slammed
his coffee cup on the bar.

Anya shot a worried glance between the two of
them, then slipped out from behind the bar and disappeared.

"I know. I just like to see you get all hot under the
collar when I call it foot lotion." Clementine flashed
him a syrupy-sweet smile and finished off her delicious coffee. She didn't ordinarily consume hot
beverages so quickly. Then again, she'd never before
had one that tasted like a liquid s'more.

Ben let out a frustrated grunt and dropped his
head in his hands.

Clementine wondered if he would notice if she
stole the remains of his coffee. He most certainly
didn't need any more caffeine. "Don't grunt at me.
You deserve it. All I did was ask a simple question."

He took a deep breath and spoke with exaggerated
calmness. "I apologize. It's just the thought of your
running around with a loaded gun…you could kill
yourself." He shook his head and closed his eyes.

"Anyway, you don't need to worry about the bears. They can't hurt you."

She eyed the stuffed grizzly with suspicion. How the dogs could curl up right underneath it and sleep was beyond her. "Why not?"

"Because it's winter." The corners of his lips turned up into that charming lopsided grin of his. Finally. "They're hibernating."

"Oh." Heat settled in Clementine's cheeks. "I suppose you're going to take back what you said earlier about how I was starting to sound like a real Alaskan."

"No, I'll cut you some slack." His smile grew a bit wider. "But can I ask you something?"

"Sure." Like she could say no after making an idiot out of herself.

His blue eyes searched hers and he asked, "What brought you here? I know you're a dog lover and you're volunteering for the race as part of your job. But they could have sent anybody. I get the feeling this is about more than just work. Why here? Why now?"

"I'm not sure I can explain my reasoning." Clementine's throat tightened. It was a loaded question to be sure. "The last time I tried to explain it to a man, he didn't understand."

She thought for a moment about the day she'd finally told Mark she couldn't marry him, that he seemed more like a brother to her than a husband.

He didn't understand that, either. She doubted if he ever would.

"Try me." Ben's voice was laced with an unexpected vulnerability that broke down Clementine's resistance.

"I've lived in the same city my whole life. I've worked in the same cubicle since I took my job at *Nature World* over ten years ago. I've never taken more than one day of vacation at a time. Until yesterday, I'd never even been on an airplane." She held her breath and waited for her words to sink in. She fully expected his expression to change to one of shock, or worse, sympathy. She looked down at her hands gripping the edge of the bar, afraid that when she looked back up, he would have that same baffled expression she'd seen on Mark's face when she'd given him back his ring.

At last she looked up and met Ben's gaze. She saw no trace of pity there, or judgment. So she continued. "After practically begging for this assignment, my boss finally relented and agreed to send me here last year. When I told my fiancé about it, he was horrified."

Ben's gaze flitted ever so briefly to her left hand.

"So I stayed home." After all this time, it was almost shameful to admit. "Mark and I had grown up next door to one another. We were childhood friends and high school sweethearts. I think when he asked me to marry him, I said yes because it was what everyone expected us to do. It felt comfortable.

Safe. It took me a while to realize that marriage…
love…isn't about being safe. I mean, love should be
life's greatest adventure, right?"

Ben's expression grew pensive and he nodded
slowly. "I suppose it should."

"I have a favorite Bible verse, one that I memo-
rized as a child. John 10:10, 'I have come that they
may have life, and have it to the full.'" Clementine's voice trembled with emotion. "Do you have
any idea how many photographs I've seen from this
race? The dogs always look so happy, so free. That's
what God wants for me. I'm finally going to reach
out and take it."

"So you came to Alaska." It was a statement, not
a question.

A thoughtful silence settled between them.
Clementine should have been embarrassed. Surely
Ben didn't need to know her whole life story. He'd
probably only been making polite conversation when
he'd asked her why she was here. But for some reason, she was glad she'd told him the truth. Even
though she thought she detected a flicker of pain in
his gaze when she mentioned the Bible.

This had already proven to be a most unusual
date anyway. She doubted he would ever ask her
for a second one, no matter how she answered his
question. Even if he did, she wasn't sure she would
accept.

When he spoke, though, he didn't seem over-
whelmed by her bare honesty. He didn't look at her

like she was nuts, either. "Well, you came to the right place."

She blinked up at him. "I did?"

"Sure. Alaska has always been a place for people who crave more from life. There's nowhere else like it on earth. People come here from all over the world, searching for a new beginning. Usually, they find it." Despite his words of hope, Ben's features were still tinged with sadness.

Clementine recognized the haunted look in Ben's crystal-blue eyes. It was one she'd seen looking back at her in her bathroom mirror. A look filled with longing. "Now can *I* ask you something?"

He gave her a meager smile. "I suppose that's only fair."

She chose her words with care. "What about the people who are already here? Where do they go to start over?"

He stared down into his coffee cup. "That's a good question. I'll let you know the answer as soon as I figure it out."

Chapter Four

Ben slept in fits and spent most of the night tangled in his bedsheets. Every time he flipped over or pounded his fist into his pillow, Kodiak sighed and crept closer to the foot of the hotel bed. When Ben at last gave up, propped himself against the headboard and aimed the remote control at the room's small television, Kodiak hopped off the bed altogether and settled in a ball on the floor.

Ben cast him a sympathetic glance. "Sorry, bud."

He knew he shouldn't feel sorry for the husky. Kodiak was a sled dog. Not too many years had passed since he slept outside, on a bed of straw, surrounded by the other members of Ben's dog team. Ben himself sometimes slept alongside them, wrapped in a thermal sleeping bag.

He'd never been the type of musher to leave his dogs unattended when they were out on the trail.

The television droned in the background, capturing his attention, exactly as he'd hoped it would. He stared at the flickering images of herds of wild musk oxen. With their woolly coats and curved horns, they looked almost prehistoric, even to a lifelong Alaskan like himself.

He'd landed on the hotel's special Alaskan channel. Designed for tourists, it played a continuous loop of educational programming about the state's history and wildlife. He supposed it was as good a channel as any. Maybe it would bore him to sleep.

Unlikely, with the thoughts that had kept him awake much of the night still tormenting him. Thoughts very un-Alaskan in nature.

Thoughts of Clementine Phillips.

Specifically, thoughts of her shoes.

She wouldn't last half a minute as a dog handler in those glorified bedroom slippers. Once she grabbed hold of the gang line and felt the power of the dog team, her feet would slide right out from under her. If she was really intent on her plans— and it looked as though no amount of lecturing on Ben's part would stop her—he was going to have to do something about those shoes.

Stay out of it. This isn't your problem.

Clementine was a tourist. Whether she slid down the chute on her backside shouldn't mean a thing to Ben. By this time next week, she would be gone.

Then why can't I stop thinking about her?

Ben hadn't given a second thought to romance in as long as he could remember. In his mushing days, there simply hadn't been time. And since then, he'd walked around in a perpetual state of numbness, as though the frostbite in his hands on that long-ago night had somehow found its way to his heart.

Even if he did want to start a relationship with someone, it certainly wouldn't be with a tourist who believed God had sent her here on some kind of divine adventure mission. Her unabashed thirst for life was alarming enough, even without the mention of the God who Ben had done his best to forget over the past four years.

So, he told himself, his concern for Clementine had nothing to do with romance. Thoughts of that nature would never have entered his mind if she hadn't told him about her former fiancé—a complete idiot, in Ben's opinion.

He pushed from his mind the image of her laughing, with snow clinging to the ringlets surrounding her face. He refused to think about her emerald eyes. Or the way her warm smile seemed to melt the block of ice surrounding his heart.

Instead, he focused on the shoes.

The shoes he could deal with.

Clementine almost didn't hear her cell phone ringing, even though she'd been awake for at least an hour. After her morning devotional, she'd become mesmerized by a television show about musk oxen.

In honor of her trip, she'd changed her ring tone to barking dogs. This was, perhaps, not the best idea when traveling to a destination packed with happy, barking huskies. Already, she could hear dogs outside, howling for their breakfast.

She realized she must be getting a call when Nugget cocked her head and yapped at the cell phone, perched on the edge of the night table.

"Here, baby." Clementine handed Nugget the moose-shaped dog toy she'd picked up in the lobby gift shop.

With her dog appeased, she picked up the cell phone. Fully prepared to see the familiar *Nature World* phone number on the screen, she cleared her throat and tried to remember the state of the papers strewn about her cubicle.

But the call wasn't from her office. An unfamiliar number, preceded by the 907 Aurora area code, flashed on the screen.

"Hello?" she answered, as she gave Nugget's moose toy a gentle tug.

"Hi, is this Clementine?" That rugged voice could only belong to one person.

She sat up straighter and abandoned the game of tug-of-war with her dog. "Yes."

"This is Ben Grayson." He cleared his throat and added, "You know, Kodiak's dad."

She knew, of course, exactly who Ben Grayson was. But his embellishment brought a smile to her lips. "Good morning, Ben."

"I hope you don't mind that I'm calling. I got your number from the race volunteer directory."

"I don't mind." The way her heartbeat kicked up a notch told her this was an understatement.

"I was wondering…" Ben paused and Clementine held her breath, wondering if he was going to ask her out again.

She'd enjoyed their coffee date. And the bittersweet look on his face when he'd spoken about starting over told her there was more to Ben than met the eye. The possibility of getting to know him better intrigued her. Probably more than it should have, considering she had only a handful of days to spend in Alaska. Not to mention the fact that she wasn't remotely ready for any kind of romantic relationship.

"Are you busy this morning?"

Clementine tightened her grip on her cell phone. "I have my dog handling class this afternoon, but I'm free until then."

Her mind raced with possibilities of what he might be thinking. Something adventurous probably. Snowshoeing? Or maybe a nice, scenic drive through the mountains. She'd heard there was a glacier nearby.

Then, in his manly tone that made Clementine picture a mountain man on the other end of the line, he asked, "How would you like to do some shopping?"

Shopping? Her gaze flitted to the ceiling. *Lord, is he serious?*

Before she had a chance to answer, Ben sighed. "I'll be honest. I have an ulterior motive."

Clementine furrowed her brow and gathered Nugget, complete with moose, in her lap. This was not sounding good. "What would that be exactly?"

"If you're going to handle dogs at the start of the race, you need some better shoes. It's a matter of safety."

"You're concerned for my safety?" *Oh no, not again.* At least he'd abandoned the foot lotion idea. It was progress. Sort of.

"Yes. I was thinking about it earlier and I'd like to help."

"You were thinking about me?" She knew she shouldn't have blurted it out like that, but she couldn't resist. Sort of like the snowball she'd thrown at his head.

He was silent for a moment. "I guess I was," he finally admitted, although he didn't sound remotely pleased about it.

Clementine wondered if the invitation was really part of some elaborate conspiracy to drag her into the world of foot lotion, or maybe even to keep her away from the hotel long enough to miss her dog handling class. Well, she wasn't about to fall for such trickery. She opened her mouth with every intention of saying no.

Instead she found herself saying, "Shopping sounds great."

They met in the lobby an hour later, with Kodiak and Nugget in tow. Ben ordered two flavored coffees with extra whipped cream without any prompting from Clementine.

"You remembered." She smiled as he handed her a cup of turtle caramel latte, the special of the day.

"I've never heard anyone order coffee with extra whip. It's kind of hard to forget." He looked down at his own cup, towering with a giant dollop of whipped cream. "Especially after I tasted it for myself."

She sipped her drink. She wouldn't have believed it could taste better than the toasted marshmallow coffee the day before, but it did. "Mmm. This one tastes like a candy bar."

"Candy bar for breakfast. I aim to please." His lips hitched into a grin.

Clementine could see his dimples, winking at her, through his beard. "Have you always had a beard? It seems as though everyone here has one."

Ben ran his free hand over his strong jawline as they walked toward the revolving doors. "I guess I've had it for most of my adult life. This is short, though. It barely qualifies."

"Look at that one." She pointed to a Gold Rush Trail poster, propped on an easel by the registration desk. The poster featured a close-up photograph of a musher with a thick, heavy beard, dripping with icicles. "Beards must be an Alaskan thing."

"Actually, they're more of a keeping-warm thing." Ben gave the poster an almost wistful once-over before looking back down at his coffee.

"Does it work?"

"The beard?" He laughed. "I guess you could say it does."

Ben pushed the door open for her and she stepped outside. The cold air bit at her nose and her teeth chattered.

"Maybe I should try growing one, although I'm not sure I could pull it off." She lifted her chin. "What do you think?"

He reached toward her and cupped her chin with a gentle graze of his fingertips. "I think you look beautiful just the way you are."

His hand was rough, masculine. Clementine grew instantly warm despite the snow flurries swirling in the wind. In fact, she experienced an almost-melting sensation in her limbs. "So no beard, then?"

Ben frowned and pulled away so quickly that Clementine wondered if she had only just imagined the unexpected tenderness of the moment. "No beard."

The pleasant warmth coursing through her cooled. For that, Clementine was grateful. Falling for Ben Grayson wasn't part of her plan for her trip to Alaska. She took a step and fell—literally—into Ben's solid chest.

"Here, hold on to me." Ben hitched her dog carrier farther up on her shoulder before tucking her arm through his. "Let's go get you some new shoes."

They walked arm-in-arm through the streets of downtown Aurora, sipping their coffee, with Kodiak trotting out in front. A comfortable silence settled between them. Every so often, Clementine sneaked a look at Ben. Once or twice, she found him watching her as well.

His words resonated in her mind. *I think you look beautiful just the way you are.* And she realized she *felt* beautiful. She wondered if it was because she'd finally come to the realization that God wanted more for her life. Or maybe it had something to do with the man walking beside her. She couldn't be sure, but she preferred the first option.

"Here we are." Ben patted her arm and pulled her to a halt. Kodiak paused as well and looked back at them. "Are you ready to try on some shoes?"

Clementine took in the yellow Army Surplus sign in the shop window in front of her, as well as the mannequins dressed in army fatigues. She looked down at her own faux fur-trimmed parka and glanced back at Ben. "You're joking, right?"

"Trust me."

She eyed the sly smile on his well-formed lips with suspicion. "It's hard to trust you when you're smirking."

"I'm not smirking," he said with a smirk.

"Yes, you are."

"I'm sorry. I can't help it. You just look so traumatized at the idea of shopping here." His smirk morphed into an ear-splitting grin.

Maybe he really was joking after all. "So we're going somewhere else?"

"Nope." His lips twitched, obviously in an effort to keep a straight face. "Trust me. Your feet will stay warm and you'll stop slipping and sliding all over the place."

"Okay." She sighed and cast a fond farewell glance toward her pink boots, although she had to admit they weren't at all practical. Ben was right. She'd never be able to handle sled dogs—or much else, for that matter—in these shoes.

They tossed their empty coffee cups in the trash can outside. Ben gave Kodiak a down command and ordered him to stay put. The husky watched with his warm gold eyes as Ben led Clementine into the store with a protective hand on her elbow.

He ushered her to the front counter where a bored-looking young man glanced up at them from his newspaper. "Can I help you?"

"You sure can." Ben smiled, his dimples flashed and he looked a bit too pleased for Clementine's taste.

Trust him.

He slid his gaze toward Clementine and winked.

The wink floated through her, like a snowflake on a soft breeze.

Then Ben turned his attention back toward the sales clerk. "We need some bunny boots."

"Did you say bunny boots?" Clementine's voice rose an octave, her eyes glimmered with surprise and she glanced down at Nugget, snoozing away in the confines of her dog carrier.

Where, no doubt, the dog's pint-sized paws were encased in those crazy bunny slippers.

"Don't get too excited." Her delighted reaction caused a definite stir in Ben's heart. "They don't have ears."

"I didn't think they had ears." Her cheeks took on a pleasant rosy hue.

Ben wasn't sure he believed her. Ears or not, she willingly gave the kid behind the counter her size. While he disappeared to the stockroom, Clementine shrugged out of her parka and situated herself on a bench. Once Nugget's dog carrier was settled next to her feet, she removed her pink suede slippers. Ben couldn't help but notice her socks were pink as well.

Of course.

All the while, Ben watched her, counting the seconds and waiting for her to break.

One…two…three.

"Okay, I'll bite." She threw her hands up. "What are bunny boots?"

Ben raised his brows in appreciation. "Three seconds. Wow, you held out longer than I expected."

"I'm a pretty patient person."

"Good." He nodded. "That will serve you well later on this afternoon at your handling class."

She narrowed her gaze at him, but he could see the slight flicker of nerves cross her features. Good. He hoped she was nervous. Nervous enough to skip the class and give the paw ointment proposition a fair amount of consideration.

Her glare intensified. "Are you going to tell me or not?"

Maybe she wasn't nervous. It must have been wishful thinking on his part. "They aren't actually called bunny boots. That's just a widely used nickname."

"For?"

"For extreme cold weather vapor boots. They were originally designed by the army for military use." He nodded toward the fatigue-clad mannequins in the window.

"Hence the army surplus store."

"They're quite popular now among civilians, here and in other arctic regions. Mushers wear them all the time. Nothing on earth will keep your feet warmer."

She lit up again, obviously pleased at the prospect of fitting in with the mushing world. "So how did they get their nickname?"

"Have you ever heard of the snowshoe rabbit?" He doubted it. The rabbit wasn't a common resident of the Lower Forty-Eight. And he was certain one had never set foot—or was it paw?—as far south as Texas.

Foot. Rabbits have feet. Not paws.

Good grief, he was already starting to sound like her.

He allowed himself a moment to look at her—really look—and let his gaze see past the mass of curls dusted with a fine layer of snow, the dainty, upturned nose reddened from the cold, and the lady-like way she crossed her feet at the ankles. Instead, he took in the fiery sparkle in her luminous green eyes. Even though he'd known her only a few short days, he knew exactly what that expression meant.

For Clementine Phillips, this trip was no ordinary vacation. She was in Alaska looking for a life-changing adventure.

Ben couldn't say why, but he'd taken it upon himself to make sure whatever adventure she managed to find was life-*changing,* not life-*ending.* The bears might be hibernating, but Alaska was full of other dangers she knew nothing about.

Ben's sleepless night had convinced him he couldn't leave her to her own devices. He hadn't a clue how he would do it, but he would make sure she left the state in one, uninjured piece. The reasons behind this decision were purely selfish—he was looking for absolution.

He couldn't change the past, but maybe he could somehow change the future.

She grinned at him and let one of her pink slippers dangle from her toe. The sparkle in those wide eyes intensified, and Ben's temple throbbed.

Clearly he had his work cut out for him.

"Actually, I know all about snowshoe rabbits." She raised a brow at him, and a proud gleam took the place of the dangerous twinkle in her eyes.

Ben would have been relieved if he hadn't known its disappearance was only temporary. "You do?"

"I certainly do." She checked off a few pertinent facts. "They earned the name snowshoe because of the tracks their large hind feet leave in the snow. And their fur changes color with the seasons, from brown in the spring and summer to snowy white in the winter. This change helps them blend in with the surroundings and hide from predators."

Ben should have been annoyed, and probably would have been if it had been anyone else who had caught him off guard like that. He wasn't annoyed, though. In fact, quite the opposite. "I'm impressed."

"They're hunted by foxes, weasels, owls and coyotes. But bobcats, in particular, find them to be a delicacy." She sighed. "I had to research them for a story the magazine did last year on *leporids*."

Ben shook his head. He didn't know the part about the bobcats. He also had no idea what leporid meant but he wasn't about to ask. "We don't have leopards in Alaska."

"*Leporid*. It comes from the Latin for hare." She tilted her head and blinded him with another smile.

"Does it now?" He crossed his arms. "Because you seem to be an expert on such things, you should probably be able to figure out why they're called bunny boots, Miss Smarty-Pants."

The sales clerk returned from the back room holding a pair of white rubber boots, with their traditional bulbous toes.

"They're white!" Clementine let her dangling pink

shoe fall the rest of the way to the floor. "Just like the snowshoe hare's feet. How perfectly adorable."

Ben tried to remember the last time he'd heard anyone describe bunny boots as *adorable* and came up empty. He'd always thought they were flat-out ugly. Ugly but warm. "Try them on and see if they fit."

She slid into the shoes and pranced up and down the center aisle of the store as if she were in some kind of fashion show.

Her delight even brought a hint of a smile to the bored-to-death clerk. He shrugged. "We also have the Mickey Mouse boots, if you'd prefer those."

Clementine straightened from where she'd bent down to check on Nugget, snoozing away in the dog carrier. "Mickey Mouse boots? What are those?"

"They're basically the same as the bunny boots, only they're black." The clerk gestured toward the stockroom. "I could bring some out if you like."

"Black?" Clementine's brow crumpled. "Why aren't they yellow?"

"Uh?" The sales kid looked back and forth between Clementine and Ben.

Ben rolled his eyes. "Because they're black."

"That's not an answer." Clementine jammed her hands on her hips. "Mickey Mouse always wears yellow shoes. So does Minnie. Following that logic, shouldn't Mickey Mouse boots also be yellow?"

The teenaged clerk nodded in agreement. "She has a point."

Ben closed his eyes and took a deep breath. He tried his best not to think about the fact that he was standing in an army surplus store arguing about what color shoes some cartoon rodent wore, instead of sitting alone in his peaceful cabin in the woods.

When he opened his eyes, Clementine smiled sweetly at him, as if this were an entirely normal conversation.

He smiled back woodenly and decided to forgo the matter of color altogether. Because, now that he thought about it, the mouse's shoes *were* yellow. "Mickey Mouse boots aren't quite as warm."

The clerk shot Clementine a questioning look. "They're rated for temperatures down to negative twenty degrees. Aurora won't get any colder than that. You're here for the race, right? Are you here just for the start, or will you be going to Nome for the finish?"

"I'm only here for a week." The twinkle in her eyes dimmed.

Everything within Ben told him it was for the best. Nome was no place for a woman like Clementine. Its very location, on the coast of the Bering Sea, made it more than a little dangerous.

Still, it was a shame she would miss seeing the dogs cross the finish line.

Ben ground his teeth.

Keep your mouth shut. Don't say it.

"You would really enjoy Nome."

The words were quiet, barely audible. But they'd come from his own mouth.

Clementine said nothing. She looked down at the white boots on her feet, her delicate features tinged with sadness.

She was lovely. Even without her exuberant smile, she was so beautiful that Ben's heart clenched. And he had the sudden urge to kiss her, just as he had standing outside the hotel.

Ben cleared his throat. The army surplus store was hardly an appropriate place for such things. Not that kissing Clementine Phillips would ever be appropriate.

The clerk's voice broke the heavy silence. "If you're not going to Nome, either pair would be fine."

Ben didn't give her a chance to speak. "She'll take the bunny boots," he blurted.

Just in case.

He fully expected an argument from her. Or, at the very least, for her to say something sarcastic about his telling her what to do.

But she didn't. She simply nodded and reached a graceful hand toward her collarbone, where she toyed with the slender chain around her neck. Ben followed the subtle movements of her fingertips until his gaze landed on the small gold cross dangling from her necklace. A tiny reminder of yet another reason why it was for the best that Clementine went home at the end of the week.

As Ben stared at the cross, any lingering thoughts of Nome fled from his mind.

"I'll wait for you outside." He ignored the look of confusion that passed through her features as he pushed his way out the door and back out into the cold.

The sidewalk was empty, save for Kodiak. Ben rested his hand on the dog's head without bothering to pull on his gloves. He let the frigid air numb his fingertips and waited for it to once again do the same to his heart.

Chapter Five

❧

Clementine was grateful for the intimidating stack of release forms the dog handling instructor expected her to read and sign. In her ordinary life, she never would have thought phrases such as *physically demanding activity* and *injuries are not uncommon* would inspire gratitude, but she would have been wrong. Sitting in the makeshift classroom at the Northern Lights Inn, she pored over the typewritten pages. Each word, each letter was a welcome distraction from the bewilderment of shopping with Ben.

To say that the man was moody would be an understatement of Alaskan-sized proportions. The morning had started off just fine. More than fine. It had been blissful. Ben was relaxed, charming even.

And he'd told her she was beautiful.

She could still hear his voice, see his face, surrounded by tiny snow flurries as he said it.

How they had gone from that moment to walking back from the army surplus store in awkward silence was beyond her. He hadn't even tucked her arm through his, as he'd done earlier. The good news was she no longer needed to lean on him for balance. He'd been right about the bunny boots. She was perfectly fine on her own.

And isn't that what she wanted?

Yes, that's exactly what I want.

She made every effort to forget how comforting it had felt, walking through the snow-covered sidewalks arm-in-arm, and instead concentrated on the stack of papers in front of her. It was no use. All the legal mumbo jumbo did nothing but make her nervous enough to almost reconsider Ben's foot lotion offer.

Not that she would have ever admitted as much to him.

She couldn't change her mind now anyway. While she'd been shopping with Ben, her boss at *Nature World* had called. She hadn't spoken to him yet, but his voice mail was more than clear. Not only did he want her to handle dogs, but he also had a new assignment. He wanted her to learn how to mush.

She gulped.

I can do this.

"If everyone would pass me their release forms, I think we're ready to begin." The instructor, a young man who looked barely old enough to drive, stood at the front of the room.

Maybe he *wasn't* old enough to drive. Clementine supposed he could have mushed a dog team to the hotel. But he already had the requisite Alaskan beard, so she supposed he must be older than he looked.

"Thank you for volunteering as dog handlers for this year's Gold Rush Trail. The mushers couldn't get past the starting line of the race without the help of everyone in this room." He paused while Clementine and the other dog handlers looked at one another and smiled. "My name is Aidan Jackson. I mushed the race last year as a rookie and I'm back this year as a lead dog handler. I hope to teach you what you need to know to help get the dog teams to the starting line safely. That is your job as a handler. You are responsible for helping the musher get the dogs all harnessed up, keeping them under control until race time and slowing the team down until they cross the start line."

Clementine thought about Nugget, tucked safely at the foot of the bed in her hotel room. It certainly wouldn't take a team of people to get a dog like her under control. Then again, she was a Pomeranian, not an Alaskan husky.

"There's really only one thing you need to know to be a successful sled dog handler."

Clementine sat a little straighter in her chair, eager to hear this important bit of wisdom. Whatever it was, she was ready for it. Hopefully it would be enough to forever eradicate the visions of foot lotion dancing in her head.

Aidan raised his hands. His voice boomed, emphasizing the gravity of his message. "If you fall down, roll out of the way."

Clementine blinked in disbelief.

If I fall down, roll out of the way? That's it?

She felt like a five-year-old, sitting in a circle in kindergarten class. She remembered with perfect clarity the day the fireman had come to visit her classroom. How could she have forgotten? He'd brought along that striking, spotted dalmatian. Clementine had been a dog lover, even back then. And *101 Dalmatians* was her favorite movie.

Stop, drop and roll. That's what the fireman had told the class, over and over again.

Stop, drop and roll.

If you fall down, roll out of the way.

They were remarkably similar.

"If you fall down, roll out of the way," Aidan repeated. "You'll be running alongside a team of sixteen strong, athletic dogs through at least a foot of snow. Many of you will slip and fall. It might not feel so bad if you get trampled by sixteen huskies, but behind those dogs is a sled. And when the sled runs over you, it will hurt."

Clementine's throat grew dry.

Oh, dear Lord. What have I gotten myself into?

She reached for the gold cross she always wore, for reassurance.

If I fall down, roll out of the way. If I fall down, roll out of the way. If I fall down, roll out of the way.

The phrase brought her little comfort, no matter how many times she repeated it.

Then, as she wrapped her fingers around the familiar cross, other words took their place.

I can do all things through Christ, who gives me strength.

She let the holy promise soothe her nerves as Aidan explained how the dogs were harnessed and attached to the sled. As she learned the difference between a gang line, neck line and tug line, she reminded herself that the reason she was there in the first place was because God had called her to live a fuller life. He was on her side. With His help, she could do this. And if she fell down and forgot to roll out of the way, maybe He would give her the push she needed.

"Are you guys ready to head outside and get some practice?" Aidan asked.

"Yes!" A collective roar rose from the crowd of students.

Clementine's whispered "Yes, I'm ready" was lost in the animated chatter of the others as they rose and headed for the parking lot.

She filed out with the rest of them and was almost surprised when her feet didn't slip out from beneath her as she stepped onto the icy pavement.

Aidan pointed at her feet. "Nice shoes."

"Thank you." Clementine looked down at her bunny boots, which reminded her far more of Ben than any kind of *leporid.*

She looked around, hoping to see him somewhere. There were a few photographers milling around, snapping pictures of the musher trucks clustered on the side of the hotel. Not one of the newsmen in her sight had a husky trailing along. Not that Clementine would have had trouble recognizing Ben, even without Kodiak by his side.

She felt a tug of disappointment when she realized he was nowhere to be seen.

That tug was quickly forgotten when Aidan began removing dogs from his truck, one by one, and lining them up in the parking lot.

"Here, hold him, will you?" He walked toward her, hauling a cream-colored, barking dog alongside him. A dog that appeared to weigh twenty times as much as Nugget.

There was no time to hesitate. Clementine grabbed the dog's harness, right at the X above his shoulder blades. Aidan strode back to his truck, leaving her standing there, holding the dog, who was practically frothing at the mouth with excitement.

"Hey, boy." She reached her free hand toward him, with her palm up.

He stopped barking long enough to give her a wary sniff. She dropped to one knee and ran her hand under the dog's chin. To her surprise, the husky stopped barking again, craned his neck toward her and licked the side of her face.

Clementine laughed. "You silly thing. You might be an elite athlete, but you're just a regular dog at heart, aren't you?"

The dog gave her another kiss, this time accompanied by a furious wag of his tail.

"What's your name?"

Even though the dog wiggled with glee, she managed to read the name printed on his bright purple sled dog harness. "Akiak?"

"It means brave in Inuit," the volunteer handler standing behind her chimed in.

Clementine turned toward her as best she could while maintaining a firm grip on Akiak, and recognized the handler as the barista from the hotel. "Really? You know Inuit?"

She shrugged. "A little. My grandmother on my mother's side is Inupiat. Most of the Native peoples in Alaska are either Inupiat or Yupik. Both speak Inuit. So I've picked up some of the language here and there. But my grandmother would be the first one to tell you I'm by no means fluent. My dad's side of the family is Russian and I can't exactly speak that language, either. I know enough to get by."

So that's where her exotic looks come from, Clementine mused. She had hair the color of dark chocolate, but her eyes were almost violet.

"I'm Clementine, by the way."

"Extra whip. Of course. And I'm Anya." She smiled and seemed perfectly relaxed. Obviously she'd done this before. And she'd lived to tell about it.

Clementine's nerves eased somewhat with this realization.

"Don't worry. This isn't as frightening as they make it out to be. It's more fun than scary. I promise." Anya winked.

Clementine could have been embarrassed by the comment, seeing as it indicated her fear was clearly written all over her face. But any embarrassment she felt was superseded by relief. "That's good to hear. Thank you."

"Just remember—" the look in Anya's eyes turned serious "—roll out of the way if you fall down."

"Will do." Clementine tried to swallow, but the panic rising up her throat made it impossible.

She thought about asking Anya if she'd ever fallen down before when handling sled dogs and decided that maybe she didn't really want to know.

Aidan returned and, after securing Anya's dog, connected Akiak's harness to the gang line.

He showed Clementine exactly where to hold on and watched while she grabbed hold of the line. "Hang on tight now."

"I will." She tightened her grip with both hands while Akiak barked at another dog being harnessed beside him.

"They're all keyed up because they know we're about to go for a ride." Aidan ruffled the fur on the scruff of Akiak's neck before turning his attention back to Clementine. "I'm going to hop on the sled and give the Hike command. Once I do, the dogs will take off. You and the other handlers will pull back on the gang line and try to slow the team down until I tell them to stop. This is exactly what you'll be doing on race day. Now, what's the most important thing to remember once the dogs start moving?"

Panic beat against Clementine's rib cage with fast, furious wings.

I can do all things through Christ who gives me strength.

She glanced down at Akiak. A gorgeous cream-colored husky who bore the Native name for brave.

Make me brave, Lord.

"Do you remember what we talked about in class?" Aidan looked at her with expectation shining in his youthful eyes.

He couldn't be a day over nineteen, beard notwithstanding. Clementine chose to ignore the fact that all her training was coming from someone barely old enough to vote. "Stop, drop and roll."

"Uh?"

"Oops." Her cheeks burned. She thought she heard a snowflake sizzle when it landed on her skin. "I mean, if I fall down, roll out of the way."

"That's right!"

He moved on down the line, giving all the other dog handlers a similar, last-minute quiz. When he reached the end and hopped up on the sled runners, Clementine's heart leaped straight to her throat.

I can do all things through Christ who gives me strength.

She squeezed the gang line with all her might and whispered in Akiak's ear, "We can do this. You and I will be brave together."

Akiak gazed back at her with eyes so blue that they were almost translucent. Then Aidan's sharp Hike command pierced the air. The husky became nothing more than a barking, whirling blur of quick-moving paws. The raw power of the dog team lifted Clementine clear off her feet and, for the first time in her life, she knew what it felt like to fly.

Ben slumped on the bed in his hotel room and tried to ignore the mournful whine coming from Kodiak's direction. He'd already closed the thick, blackout curtains in an effort to plunge the room into dark silence. But curtains were no match for a team of howling, wound-up sled dogs. If he really wanted to drown out the sound of the dog handling class outside, he supposed he should turn on the television.

He glanced at the darkened screen and groaned inwardly. He couldn't take any more facts about musk oxen. Or the Gold Rush. Or anything else Alaskan, for that matter. The way things were going, he'd probably stumble across a documentary about snowshoe rabbits.

Was everything in the state destined to remind him of Clementine?

It appeared so. He didn't know how she did it—within days of stepping off the plane she'd somehow come to embody the very nature of Alaska. Independent, free-spirited, a bit untamed. And yet, she still had a sweet, vulnerable quality about her.

Ben found it an oddly stirring combination.

His stomach churned.

He'd fixed her shoe problem, so he really had no reason to see her until race day. But he knew he would. He'd barricaded himself in his hotel room simply to stop himself from wandering over to check out her dog handling class. At least he had the common sense to avoid that scene. He honestly didn't think he could take watching a team of dogs drag her around the parking lot.

As if her adventurous streak wasn't enough to drive him insane, there was another matter. The matter of her faith.

He pictured her delicate fingers, touching the gold cross as it lay in the subtle dip between her collar bones. It wasn't the first time he'd noticed her toying with the necklace. She'd done it the day before when she'd told him why she'd come to Alaska and quoted the Bible.

What was that verse again? Something about living life to the fullest.

The churning in Ben's gut intensified. His fingers itched. He clenched and unclenched his fists, certain the sensation was yet another lingering effect of the frostbite from the accident.

Somewhere in the back of his mind, he knew better. He was in a hotel room. He knew there was a Bible in the top drawer of the nightstand. Even if he hadn't pushed it aside to make more room for his socks, he would have known it was there. Wasn't there a Bible in every hotel room on the planet?

He pushed himself up and let his restless fingers open the drawer.

Sure enough, there it was. Red, with gold lettering in the bottom-right corner.

Ben swung his legs over the side of the bed and sat, staring at the book. Kodiak lumbered over and rested his chin on Ben's knee. The husky blinked at him, as if waiting for something.

"What?" Ben's gaze darted back and forth between the dog and the red book.

Curiosity got the best of him. He dragged the Bible to his lap and flipped it open. A few years had passed since he'd opened a Bible, but he still knew how to find a specific verse.

Four. It's been four years.

Exactly.

His fingers trembled, shaking the wisp-thin pages as he flipped to the Gospel of John. He found the tenth chapter quickly, and scanned the page for the words Clementine had quoted over coffee.

"Here it is."

Kodiak cocked his head at the sound of Ben's voice.

The verse was close to the bottom of the page, and it was printed in red letters. "I come that they may have life, and have it to the full."

A slow smile came to his lips. If anything, Clementine was certainly full of life.

He knew little of her life back home, but he remembered her mentioning working in a cubicle. He found that increasingly hard to believe.

When he reread the verse, he realized it contained another sentence. Also in red, it preceded the one that was Clementine's favorite.

Ben whispered the verse in its entirety. "'The thief comes only to steal and kill and destroy; I have come that they may have life, and have it to the full.'"

A bitter taste rose to the back of his throat. He allowed himself to remember all the reasons why he'd buried the Bible below his socks, why one could no longer be found on the bookshelves in his cabin. His life, and everything it had once been, had been destroyed. He remembered the panic, the scraping of sled runners against the ice. And, most of all, the cold.

He shook his head and slammed the book shut.

When he'd needed God most of all, he hadn't found life. In fact, he'd found the opposite.

Steal, kill, destroy.

Death and destruction. Those had been the answers to Ben's prayers that night. Not life.

Kodiak whined and nudged his chin more firmly against Ben's knee. Ben met the dog's gaze again.

The husky's eyes sparkled gold, the color of the precious mineral for which the dog sled race was named. As Ben searched those eyes, another truth hit him square in the chest.

"You lived." He laid his palm on the top of Kodiak's head. Cold fingers met warm fur. "I didn't lose everyone that night. You're still here."

Kodiak's tail thumped against the bed.

"That's right, isn't it, boy?" Ben still gripped the red book with his other hand. "We're still alive. You and me."

Ben knew whether he truly lived was debatable. He hated to think what Clementine would have to say about the matter.

At that moment, just as her name came to him, a siren pierced the air. Kodiak jerked his head away from Ben's grasp and barked. Once, twice, three times. Then he began pacing the small room and howling at the sorrowful wail of the siren.

Ben flew to the window and threw open the blackout curtains to find an ambulance approaching the hotel. It slowed as it pulled up beside a crowd of people next to a sled. The dogs harnessed to the sled had their ears pricked back and their tails hung between their legs.

The blood in Ben's veins turned to ice. The ambulance was there for someone at the dog handling class. He should have known.

What had he been doing, sitting here reading the

Bible, when he should have been making sure Clementine was safe?

He tossed the red book back in the drawer and slipped on his parka. In a firm voice, he told Kodiak to stay before he slammed the door behind him and sprinted to the parking lot. Then another word rose to his throat and stuck there. Too filled with dread to attempt to speak, Ben screamed the word in his thoughts.

Please.

Chapter Six

Despite his desperate plea, Ben fully expected to see Clementine's halo of blond curls splayed on the ice when he reached the figure curled on the ground next to the ambulance. Confusion, mixed with a surprising sense of relief, washed over him as he stared down at a man holding his arm to his chest.

A man, not a woman. Not Clementine.

The man winced as a paramedic turned his arm ever so slightly. Ben, at once feeling very out of place, looked down at his feet. He looked up only when he heard a familiar, melodic voice calling his name.

"Ben?"

He turned to see Clementine standing beside a striking, fawn-colored dog. She waved at him with one hand and held on to the dog's purple harness with the other.

Ben went to her. When he reached her, he stood

wordlessly before her, letting his gaze travel over her exquisite, unharmed face.

"You're white as a sheet." Her hat had fallen off, leaving her curls whipping in the frigid wind. She looked wild.

Ben found himself wishing he had his camera. He even reached for it, but of course it wasn't there. He hadn't even taken the time to grab his gloves on his way out the door.

He plunged his hands in his pockets. "I heard the ambulance and, um…"

"You assumed I was the one who got hurt." She lifted an angry eyebrow.

He opened his mouth to contradict her, but she wouldn't let him get a word out.

"You think I'm utterly incapable, don't you?" She huffed out a breath. "For your information, Clark over there fell down and broke his wrist. It could have happened to anyone. It's slippery out here, you know. He even stopped, dropped and rolled."

Ben's mouth twitched and he struggled not to laugh. "He rolled out of the way?"

"Yes." She nodded, and a flicker of pleasure passed through her features before she resumed her hands-on-hips, irritated stance. "You knew what I meant. When I said that earlier, my instructor looked at me like I was nuts."

"I don't think you're nuts." He took note when the husky at her feet leaned against her legs and nuzzled her knee.

She's even managed to charm the dogs.

"But you *do* think I'm incompetent." Her green eyes flashed. Glistening emeralds against the snowy white landscape.

"Far from it." He snorted. "I think you're many things, but incompetent isn't one of them."

"Silly, then?"

"No, not silly, either." He chose the first adjective that came to mind. "I was thinking more along the lines of *brave.*"

"Brave?" She eyed him with skepticism. "You say that like it's a bad thing."

He shrugged. "Not bad, necessarily. Just…"

Just what? Worrisome? Dangerous? Maddening? All of the above.

She ignored his pause and her lips curved into a smile of obvious pleasure. "You seriously think I'm akiak?"

"You've learned Inuit? Since this morning?" He wouldn't put it past her. If anyone was up to such a challenge, it would be her.

"Anya taught me." Clementine laughed and nodded toward the woman behind her.

Anya waved. "Hi, Ben."

"Anya." Ben nodded in recognition.

He'd known the barista a long time. Since *before.* Despite its grand size, Alaska was made up of small communities. He searched her face, wondering if she'd told Clementine anything about his past. Anya dropped her gaze to the dog at her feet and Ben exhaled a relieved sigh. That subtle gesture told him everything he needed to know. The accident was his story to tell. No one else's.

"And this—" Clementine continued as she gestured to the husky beside her "—is Akiak. Ben, meet Akiak. Akiak, Ben."

Ben offered a hand and Akiak plopped his paw in it.

Ben dutifully shook the dog's paw. "I suppose you taught this dog how to shake in between laps around the parking lot?"

"Now you give me too much credit." She lifted a gloved hand and swept the side of his face with her fingertip. "Your color is coming back."

Her delicate finger left a warm trail down the side of his face. "For the record, I didn't exactly assume you were the one who was hurt. I feared it was you. It's not quite the same thing."

"I suppose it's not." She removed her hand from his face and somehow Ben knew she would bring it to her throat.

The gold chain with the cross was safely tucked inside her parka, but he knew the meaning behind her subconscious gesture.

"I have issues with God." The confession came flying out of his mouth before he could stop it. He looked around, a little too late, to make sure none of the other dog handlers were listening. Thankfully, everyone seemed much more interested in Clark and his broken wrist than the state of Ben's soul. Even

Anya had wandered toward the ambulance with her assigned dog in tow.

Clementine didn't say a word. She didn't seem at all shocked or embarrassed, though. Her silence was a thoughtful one.

Ben took a deep breath. He'd already put himself out there. In fact, he'd already been more honest with her than he had with anyone else. Perhaps even himself. "Clearly your faith is an important part of your life. We're…friends. I thought you should know where I'm coming from."

"Where exactly are you coming from?" she asked in a gentle tone.

"Anger." He squeezed the hand-warmer packets in his pockets. "I guess you could say I'm angry with God."

She nodded. "Anger. I suppose that's the root of all this paranoia?"

"I'm not paranoid. I'm concerned for your safety. There's a difference."

"You're afraid."

Ben glared at her. So hard that she winced. Guilt pricked at the edges of his anger, and Ben almost wished she'd been wearing her pink slippers so she couldn't run the opposite direction. He wouldn't blame her a bit if she did.

She didn't run. She stayed right where she was, holding the dog's harness and tapping her bunny boot–clad foot. "I suppose there's never going to be a good time to tell you this, so I might as well do it now."

It was then that Ben realized the foot tapping wasn't a sign of irritation. She was nervous about something. And that *something*—whatever it was— terrified Ben to the core.

What on earth was she planning now? Ice climbing? Extreme snowmobiling?

He frowned and ground out, "What is it?"

The foot tapping ceased and she squared her shoulders. "Calm down."

"Clementine…" He exhaled a weary sigh.

"My boss wants me to learn how to mush."

Ben's blood boiled, hotter than a thousand hand-warmer packets.

Before he could spit out one word of protest—and he had plenty of them at the ready—she held up a hand to stop him. "Don't worry. Aidan Jackson has agreed to teach me."

Ben's head whipped toward Aidan and back to Clementine, fast enough to give him whiplash. "What?"

She dropped her gaze. With it, some of the sass dropped from her voice as well. "Aidan Jackson. He taught my dog handling class."

Ben snorted in frustration. "I know who he is."

Ben had covered him for the paper in the last race. He'd been a rookie. Little more than a boy. Ben didn't have a problem with *him*. But to say he had a problem with Aidan teaching Clementine how to mush was an understatement. He didn't want her anywhere near a pair of sled runners, no matter who was propping her up there.

Clementine was either oblivious to Ben's aggravation or chose to ignore it. Probably the latter. She struck him as the type of woman who stuck to her guns once her mind was made up. "Aidan offered to take a group of the dog handlers out tomorrow and teach us how to mush a team. I think it sounds amazing. And besides, my boss told me to make it happen. So this works out nicely. I just thought you should know."

Ben shook his head.

No, no, no.

"I don't even know why I'm telling you this. I don't need your permission." She jammed a mitten-clad hand on her hip.

Ben knew if she weren't attached to a gang line, via Akiak, she would have stomped off and left him standing there alone. He supposed he was grateful. Who knows where she would have gone...to hitch a ride on the Bering Sea with the crew of *The Deadliest Catch?* Somewhere of the sort, no doubt.

He leveled his gaze at her until her emerald eyes softened.

She posed a question to him. "Mushing is the state sport, isn't it?"

Not at all the question he'd anticipated. "Yes."

"I don't know if Texas even has a state sport." She scrunched her brow in apparent concentration.

As frustrated as he was, Ben had the sudden urge to smooth her worry lines with his fingertips. "It's rodeo."

"What?" Her eyes widened.

"The state sport of Texas," he mumbled. "It's rodeo."

"Are you serious?"

"I sure am."

"How in the world do you know that, Know-It-All?" She gave him a playful shove with her free hand.

"Know-It-All? Me?" He rolled his eyes. "This from the woman who professes to be an expert on the snowshoe hare."

She nudged him with her elbow. "If you ever come visit me in Texas, I'm sure you'll want to learn how to rope a cow."

If you ever come visit me in Texas...

She said it as though it were a real possibility. The thought of seeing her again was enough to douse the fire in his gut that had begun burning at the mention of her learning how to mush. Although he had no idea where the cow came into the picture. "What?"

"Rodeo. The state sport of Texas. Remember?" A smile tipped her bow-shaped lips.

He laughed, despite the seriousness of the situation. "Who's going to teach me to rope a cow?"

"I haven't a clue." She shrugged. "I've never even ridden a horse. I'm only adventurous in Alaska, like the salmon."

"The salmon?"

"Wild Alaskan salmon. Emphasis on *wild*."

Ben dropped his head in his hands and groaned. "You're trying to change the subject."

"Is it working?"

"No." He glowered at her. "Don't think for a minute I've forgotten that you want Aidan Jackson to teach you how to mush a dog team."

She shrugged and her curls swished against her shoulders. "He's teaching me. Tomorrow."

Ben wanted to scream in protest right there in the crowded parking lot. More than that, he wanted to cave and tell her he'd do it. He'd teach her how to mush himself. He still had the equipment, and if he worked late tonight he'd have the time. There was the obvious dilemma of a lack of dogs. Kodiak couldn't exactly pull both of them by himself, but even that was a hollow excuse. Reggie had plenty of extra well-trained dogs over at his place.

Even as the cold fingers of fear wrapped around his heart and his head told him he didn't want to do it, couldn't do it, he found himself nodding. "Come with me instead. I know someone who can teach you."

"What?" She peered up at him through a thick fringe of lashes. "Is this a trick? Are you going to drag me away somewhere to make foot lotion instead of learn how to mush?"

He held up his hands in a gesture of surrender. "No foot lotion."

"You said *foot lotion*." She flashed him a triumphant smile.

"No, I didn't." He'd clearly said *paw ointment,* hadn't he?

"Yes, you did."

"Fine. No *foot lotion*." He sighed. "I promise."

"It will be a real mushing lesson?" Her smile widened and the tip of her nose glowed bright pink from the cold.

"Yes, a real lesson." He stopped short of telling her that he would be her instructor, deciding he would deal with that later. He could barely wrap his mind around it himself. "I'll let you get back to work here."

"I'll see you tomorrow." She wiggled her fingers in a wave that could only be described as flirty.

The gesture brought a fresh ache to his chest. It was the physical manifestation of a punctuation mark, emphasizing precisely how much trouble he was in. He'd agreed to do the one thing he swore he'd never do again—for her.

He took a few steps backward, reluctant to turn away from her.

Just as he did, he heard her call out, "Perfect love casts out fear."

It sounded familiar, probably another Bible verse. He tried to push the sentiment from his thoughts as he walked away. Still, somewhere deep inside, he held on to her parting words. Long enough for him to get back to his room and look them up in the red book buried beneath his socks.

After a few hours of sitting in front of her laptop, emailing notes about her dog handling class to one of the staff writers at *Nature World,* the warmth finally returned to Clementine's fingers. Now she understood all the stern warnings about dressing for warmth for the class. An afternoon spent outdoors in an Alaskan winter was enough to chill her to the bone.

Her feet, however, had remained toasty warm. Thanks to the bunny boots. She hated to admit that Ben was right, but the shoes had been a brilliant idea. She would tell him as much tomorrow. The admission might be tough to get out, seeing as he so stubbornly acted as though he were right about everything. But Clementine was grateful to still have feeling in her toes, so she would swallow her pride and thank him.

The thought of it was exhausting as well as humbling. Clementine yawned, searched out the clock in her tidy hotel room and realized it was nearly midnight.

No wonder. She'd been so caught up in putting the excitement of the dog handling class into words that she'd completely lost track of time.

She slipped her feet into the bunny boots again and snapped Nugget's leash onto her collar. "Come on, sweetheart, let's go outside one last time before bed."

Nugget stiffened and refused to take a step toward the door. Clementine gave her a gentle tug, but the Pomeranian braced her diminutive front legs and leaned in the opposite direction.

Clementine reached into the pocket of her parka and removed Nugget's tiny bunny slippers. She dangled one from the tip of her pointer finger. "Is this what you're waiting for?"

Nugget answered with a shrill yip and spun in a circle at the end of her leash.

"Shh. You're going to wake half the hotel." She slipped the booties on Nugget's little paws, one by one. "I wouldn't forget your bunny boots."

With Nugget's feet as warm and toasty as Clementine's, the two of them made their way to the lobby. Clementine's gaze drifted toward the coffee bar, hoping to catch a glimpse of Ben. Or perhaps Anya. But like the rest of the lobby, it was empty, save for the stuffed bison head, which someone had decorated with an official Gold Rush Trail baseball cap.

The stab of disappointment she felt as she gazed at the lonely coffee bar worried Clementine almost as much as getting run over by a sled had worried her at dog handling class. In fact, she might even prefer getting run over by a sled to having her heart run over by another overly protective man. Toasty toes aside, Clementine wasn't about to let Ben Grayson tell her what to do.

A question nagged at her consciousness as she

scooped Nugget into her arms and twirled through the revolving door out onto the sidewalk.

If the idea of Ben being concerned for your safety is so abhorrent, then why aren't you going mushing with Aidan tomorrow?

It was a question that had only one logical answer—she preferred to spend time with Ben. Even though he had looked physically ill when she told him she intended to learn how to mush, she was attracted to him. It was a fact she didn't really want to accept but was having trouble denying. Even to herself.

"Clementine."

A manly, rugged voice, *his* voice, drifted toward her through the darkness. The way it caused her insides to flutter only confirmed her suspicions. She was attracted to Ben.

Most definitely.

She turned and found him leaning against a lamppost. In the soft glow of its light, she could just make out his half smile. He looked happy and sad at the same time, which would have been a ridiculous way to describe anyone but him. He was a mystery of sorts. Angry one minute, and offering to help her learn how to mush the next.

"Ben, hi." She joined Ben in the tiny circle of light and unclipped Nugget's leash so she could tiptoe into the snow with Kodiak. "You're up late."

"It looks like we're out here for the same reason you are." He nodded toward the dogs. "I've been working. Sorting through photos, that sort of thing. So I can take some time off tomorrow for your mushing lesson."

"About that…thank you so much. I really appreciate it. And the bunny boots." The flutter in her chest intensified and she was overcome with a sudden bashfulness she hadn't felt around him before. "I mean, I know the mushing thing kind of goes against your nature."

His dimples flashed. "Against my nature?"

"You know what I mean." She struggled to find the right words. "You don't necessarily like, or approve of, adventure."

"I see." The corner of his mouth pulled up into a full-on smirk, just as it had when he'd taken her to the army surplus store.

Clementine did her best to ignore it. A tall order, to be sure, considering how annoying she found that smirk. "So tell me about your friend."

He gave her an odd look. Even in the semi-darkness, his blue eyes glistened like ice. "My friend?"

"You said you knew someone who could teach me how to mush. Who is it?"

"That would be me." He bowed. "Mr. Non-Adventurous, at your service."

She rolled her eyes. "No, seriously, who is it?"

"I'm being serious. I'm going to teach you." His wry smile told her he was enjoying the moment, but his eyes were solemn. Grave, even.

"You know how to mush?" She had to ask, but in that instant, she knew it was true.

He nodded, but his gaze shifted uneasily to the ground. "Yes, since I could barely walk. My father was a musher, and his father before him. At one time, it was almost as natural to me as breathing."

His admission stunned her into silence. He could have turned into a polar bear before her very eyes and she wouldn't have been any more surprised. Ben Grayson, the foot lotion peddler, was a third-generation musher?

She sneaked a glance at the wide set of his shoulders and the obvious muscles beneath his parka. He certainly looked like an athlete. And he shared such a close bond with his dog. She really should have known.

But it had never once crossed her mind. Not in her wildest imagination.

She eyed him with newfound curiosity. "Why haven't you told me this before?"

"It's not something I talk about."

"Why not?"

"Because it's not." He gave her a warning look that told her the topic was closed for discussion.

Clementine honored his feelings on the subject and dropped it. But she couldn't help but wonder how in the world he was going to take her mushing when he couldn't even discuss it. "Are you sure about this?"

He exhaled a tortured sigh. "No. I haven't been sure of much of anything since I met you."

This answer satisfied Clementine in a way that made her cheeks warm. "I'm going to take that as a compliment."

"You should." His tone grew soft and he leveled his gaze at her for a long, meaningful moment.

Then he whistled for Kodiak and stepped away from the lamppost and into the darkness.

"I'll see you tomorrow," she called out, before he disappeared entirely.

"Tomorrow." There was an unmistakable smile in his voice. "For mushing."

Chapter Seven

Clementine studied the menu at the coffee bar and bit her lip. She'd planned on getting a box of coffee to bring along on her mushing lesson with Ben. Apparently, wherever they were going was on the outskirts of Aurora. They had a drive ahead of them.

But the idea of plain coffee had suddenly lost its appeal.

Anya stood behind the counter and watched Clementine with amusement etched in her features. "Is there a problem?"

"Not exactly." Clementine scrunched her brow and reread the name of the special of the day. Chocolate cherry latte. Seriously? How was she supposed to resist that? "Well, sort of."

"Sort of?"

"I was hoping to get a box of coffee to go. But how I am supposed to order something plain and dreary like that when you've gone and invented something called a chocolate cherry latte?"

"That's what got you all worried?" Anya leaned forward and lowered her voice to a whisper, as if she were letting Clementine in on some sort of secret. "If that's your biggest problem, then you are one lucky girl." She laughed.

Clementine forced a smile. "That's right. Lucky me."

It wasn't her biggest problem. Not by a long shot.

She glanced at the revolving door that led to the parking lot. Any minute now, her biggest problem would be strolling inside, ready to take her mushing.

The line between friendship and something more with Ben Grayson had begun to blur before he told her that he was a musher. Clementine couldn't put her finger on exactly when, but the sparks had definitely been there. The trouble now was that those sparks were becoming more difficult to ignore.

Ben wasn't the cautious man she'd thought he was. He was a musher. Why did that suddenly make him all the more appealing?

"So what will it be?" Anya reached on the shelf behind her for one of the square cardboard boxes with a spout at the bottom that Clementine had seen her give other hotel guests who ordered large amounts of coffee to go. "Chocolate cherry lattes or a box of boring?"

"Well, when you put it like that…" Clementine laughed and the tension she'd been carrying in her shoulders eased somewhat. So she found Ben attractive? It didn't have to mean anything. She wasn't ready to trust a man with her affection. She'd tried that once, with disastrous consequences. Clementine wasn't about to make that mistake again.

"You know there's such a thing as compromise?" Anya drummed her fingers on the empty coffee box.

Clementine blinked. A compromise? That never worked. At least it hadn't with Mark. "Pardon?"

"A compromise." Anya opened the box and flipped the lever on the espresso machine. "I can make you a box of chocolate cherry-flavored coffee and throw in a generous amount of steamed milk. But I can't give you the whip you seem to love so much. It would melt before you get wherever you're going."

A compromise—the coffee. Of course. "That sounds perfect."

Anya went to work mixing together something delicious. At least Clementine assumed it was delicious, judging from the decadent aroma of cherries, milk chocolate and coffee beans wafting from behind the bar.

"Here you go." Anya slid the box toward her. "Where are you off to anyway?"

"Ben Grayson is taking me on a mushing lesson," Clementine said, loving the way it sounded. Loving it too much, she was afraid.

"Really?" Anya's brows lifted in a look of surprise. "This is definitely a special occasion. I'm glad you picked the flavored coffee. A box of boring would definitely not do. You two have a great time."

"Thanks." Clementine clutched the box of coffee to her chest and smiled.

You two have a great time.

They were going off on an Alaskan adventure. How could they not? Clementine would forget about those pesky sparks, at least for now. Besides, dog mushing didn't exactly sound like a romantic activity. Her heart would be safe. She was sure of it.

"Are you sure you're ready for this?" Ben stole a glance at Clementine in the passenger seat and realized it was a ridiculous question. Excitement bounced off her in waves. She was a firecracker, ready to explode.

"Of course." She looked over her shoulder, once again, at the empty backseat. "I wish you would tell me where the dogs are. And the sled, for that matter. Are we really going mushing? Or is this just an elaborate kidnapping to prevent me from going with Aidan's group?"

"Kidnapping?" He pretended to consider the idea. "I hadn't considered such drastic measures. I have to admit the thought carries great appeal."

She frowned, or made a valiant effort to. Her joy was inextinguishable. "You're taking me mushing. You promised."

"Yes, I did." God help him.

He'd spent the day getting everything in order. Moving the dogs, checking the sled, untangling the spiderweb of lines. His equipment was still in surprisingly good condition. Despite years of neglect, it was all good to go. The only thing he was lacking was the most important ingredient—a dog team.

Reggie had been more than accommodating in that regard. Ben was certain his friend must have been stunned to find him standing on his front porch first thing in the morning, asking to borrow a few second-string dogs. If he was shocked, he'd hidden it well. They'd walked the yard together, debating which of the huskies would be best for a leisurely evening ride, as if such a thing was a common occurrence. As if Ben dropped by and borrowed dogs on a regular basis.

Despite Reggie's nonchalance, by the time Ben had loaded five eager dogs into his truck and backed out of the driveway, his friend let out a whoop of joy that could be heard clear across the Lower Forty-Eight.

He would need to make things clear with Reggie when he returned the dogs. This was a one-time thing. He was taking Clementine mushing today, but it wasn't the start of anything.

Anything at all.

He maneuvered the SUV around a curve, down a mountain road he'd traveled more times than he could count. Clementine kept her gaze glued to the scene in front of them. Frozen rivers, flanked on either side by snow-covered mountains, stretched as far as the eye could see.

"What are those?" She pointed to a series of tall poles on the side of the road.

"Avalanche markers. They're used to locate the highway in the event of a slide."

She peered at the wall of white through the windshield and gulped. "Does that happen often?"

Ben pointed to a dip between two mountains where a wide strip of snow cut a path toward the tree line. "See that area over there that looks like a ski slope?"

She squinted at it. "Yes."

"That's from an avalanche. It's a couple of weeks old. The transportation department uses explosives to set off planned avalanches whenever there's an excess of loose snow on the mountain."

"Oh." Her relief was palpable. "So we're not going to get buried in a pile of snow any minute?"

"I don't think so." He smiled, reached across the front seat for her hand and covered it with his own. "You're safe with me, Clementine."

Even as he said the words, he wondered how long they would be true. First it was dog handling. Now mushing. He hated to think what she would want to do next. His mind told him not to make promises he couldn't keep. He realized he spoke more out of his desire to protect her than from any sense of reality, but he couldn't seem to stop himself.

Her hand felt small and delicate in his. He didn't want to let it go.

"We're here," he said as they turned off the main road, down a path packed with hard snow.

The SUV crawled through a break in the evergreens until they reached a clearing. A cottage stood in the center with a red door and a stone chimney that reached toward the sky, which was beginning to glow amber in the twilight. Directly to the right, a cluster of red square boxes dotted the snow. Upon their arrival, several dogs poked their heads out of the snow-covered crimson doghouses. Kodiak sat atop his, as he'd always done back in their sledding days, watching over the yard. To Ben, his expression had always been reminiscent of a wise old owl.

Ben watched Clementine take in the scene with keen interest. He didn't realize he'd been holding his breath, hoping for a favorable reaction until her eyes widened with wonder.

"I feel like I'm in a Christmas card. It's so beautiful here, it doesn't seem real." She touched the car window with a gentle graze of her fingertips and whispered, "Where are we exactly?"

He couldn't remember the last time he'd brought someone here. Who had it been? Reggie? Perhaps. It certainly hadn't been a woman. "This is my home."

"You live here?" Clementine climbed out of the car while Ben held the door open. She shook her head. "This is your house?"

He held her mittened hand so she could get her balance in the shin-deep snow. "Yep. My father built it with his own hands. I grew up here and now I live here alone."

The word *alone* floated awkwardly between them. Ben had never thought himself lonely out here, with no one but Kodiak for company. But that was beginning to change.

"Where do your parents live now?"

"You'll love this." He gave her a wry grin. "Florida."

"Florida?" She shook her head. "No way. They left all this for Florida?"

"About ten years ago. My dad founded a mushing team down there."

She scrunched her brow. Clearly she thought he was pulling her leg. "How is that possible? It doesn't snow in Florida."

That's what Ben had thought initially. He should have known his dad would find a way. Mushing ran in the Grayson blood, he'd always said. "Instead of sleds they use carts with wheels. The dogs run in the sand."

"Incredible. Now that's something I'd like to see."

Maybe you will someday.

The idea blindsided him, and he dropped her hand before he did something ridiculous—like saying it out loud.

He'd never taken anyone home to meet his parents. Likewise, he'd never been the type to long for hearth and home. But being around Clementine was starting to awaken something in his soul. She made him want things that he'd given up on long ago.

Mushing was one thing. But romance was an entirely different matter. He'd spent four long years trying to get over the loss of his dog team. Deep down, he knew the wound he carried from their loss wasn't any closer to being healed than it had been the day they'd disappeared under the ice. He couldn't begin to imagine the pain of losing a loved one—a woman. A wife.

He wouldn't be able to live through such grief. If his past had taught him anything, it was that he was better off alone.

"Thank you for this. For today, I mean." Clementine bit her bottom lip, as Ben had noticed she always did when she was nervous.

What he hadn't noticed was how pink it was. He tried to look away from it but couldn't. "You're welcome."

"I know you don't like to talk about it, and teaching me to mush wasn't exactly on your agenda." She peered up at him with her big green eyes. Looking at them was almost as bad as looking at her lips. He could lose himself in eyes like that if he wasn't careful.

Things were getting too serious. He had to do something to lighten the mood. "Because I'm so boring and unadventurous."

She laughed and looked into his eyes, as if she

were trying to see inside of him. "What else are you hiding from me? Do you skydive?"

"No."

"Are you a storm chaser?"

"No."

"Do you like to swim with sharks?"

This one elicited a grin. "No, I prefer whales."

"Oh, that's right. This is Alaska. Whale country." Her expression grew more serious. "Do you own a gun?"

"Yes." He frowned. "As you just said, this is Alaska."

"Bear insurance. Gotcha." Her gaze flitted to the sled, waiting for them next to the dog yard. "Are you bringing it with us when we go mushing?"

Her line of questioning was beginning to unnerve him. "I told you—they're hibernating."

"There are plenty of other threats out there. What about moose? There could be a rogue mad moose in the woods somewhere." She swept her arm toward the trees.

What he needed her to do was stop talking about things that could get her killed. Sooner rather than later. "Clementine, please."

"Or caribou. What if Rudolph had a bad day and decided to take it out on some innocent people mushing through the woods?"

"Clementine," he growled.

"I think you should teach me how to use it." She smiled sweetly at him, as if she were suggesting he teach her how to make cupcakes instead of shooting a gun.

"Clementine, I'm going to get you to stop talking about this the best way I know how." He let his gaze fall to her mouth as he pulled her toward him.

She let out a little squeal, and he took her hands and wrapped them around his neck. He cupped her face, tipped her chin toward his and paused. In that sweet moment of anticipation, he gave her one last lingering look. "I'm going to kiss you now. Doesn't that sound better than learning to shoot?"

She nodded wordlessly.

And he lowered his lips toward hers.

Ben's kiss could only be described as glorious. His lips were surprisingly soft. And warm. And the way his fingertips caressed the side of Clementine's face made her feel like an exquisite treasure.

When he sighed, and the kiss grew deeper, she dazzled. All the way down to her toes.

No man has ever made me feel this way before.

She felt as though he was offering himself to her, heart and soul. All of his emotions, all the hurt of his past and hope for the future, were wrapped up in that one blinding kiss.

As phenomenal as the kiss was, she never expected to see stars. Yet she did. Quite literally.

When Ben's lips pulled away from hers, Clementine inhaled a joyous breath and opened her eyes— and there they were. Stars, glittering everywhere.

She blinked, convinced she was seeing things.

But the air was filled with shimmering bits of light. They formed a halo around Ben's head. She squinted, trying to capture at least one of them with her gaze before it flickered and disappeared.

"Clementine, are you okay?" The expression on Ben's face was an odd mix of concern and desire.

"Stars." She reached for one, but it vanished before she could touch it. "You kissed me, and now I'm seeing stars."

His mouth curved up into a smug grin, which would have normally irritated her to no end. Under the present circumstances, however, she could hardly blame him for being the tiniest bit proud of himself. It wasn't every day that a man kissed a woman and she saw stars.

Nothing even remotely close to this had ever happened when she kissed Mark.

Ben's gaze darted above her head and then farther to the left. His self-satisfied look morphed into one of amusement. "You're not seeing stars."

"Yes, I am." She most definitely was. She almost wanted them to disappear so she could ask him to kiss her again.

"No, you're not." He held out his hands, and a few of them fell toward his open palms. "This is diamond dust."

"Diamond dust?" She wasn't sure what he meant, but it sounded every bit as good as stars. Even better maybe.

"Diamond dust." He nodded. "We're in a cloud of tiny ice crystals. It happens here sometimes."

"Oh." A furious flush settled in the vicinity of her cheeks. "So you're not responsible for this?"

"I can't take credit for it." He winked. "But I certainly appreciate the assumption."

She narrowed her gaze at him, and the look in his eyes turned soft, tender. He wrapped his arms around her and pressed a gentle kiss to the top of her head. All around them, the air glittered. The beauty of it stole the breath from her lungs, and she burrowed deeper into his embrace.

Diamond dust.

He could call it whatever he wanted. As far as Clementine was concerned, Ben had kissed her and she saw stars.

As thrilling as it was, it scared the life out of her. She barely knew Ben Grayson. She couldn't start a relationship with him. She'd known Mark her whole life and look what a mess that had become. Ben was practically a stranger. She didn't want to fall for him and risk her heart again. Not now. Not when she finally had the gumption to go after what she wanted.

That being said, he was making it awfully difficult.

"Ben Grayson," she whispered into his shoulder, "who are you?"

He drew back and gazed into her eyes. "I'm the one…the man who's going to teach you how to mush a dog team."

Her heart did a little flip-flop. She glanced at the square doghouses tucked among the trees. "Now?"

"Now." He grinned. "Unless you've changed your mind."

"Not on your life."

"Your chariot awaits." He released her from the embrace, somewhat reluctantly if the look on his face was any indication.

Clementine's pulse quickened as he took her hand and led her toward the dog yard. The doghouses, with their bright red paint, looked like giant holly berries nestled in the frosty ground. Between them, tall evergreens stretched toward the sky, their boughs heavy with thick blankets of snow. She inhaled a lungful of pine-scented air.

"I can't believe you live here. Any minute I expect to see Rudolph drop from the sky."

"Again with Rudolph." Ben shook his head. "What is your fascination with him? There are other reindeer, you know."

She wiggled her eyebrows at him. "Jealous?"

"Of a reindeer?" He snorted. "I don't think so."

"I think you are. He has a shiny red nose. And he's the lead reindeer."

"But if you kissed him, would you see stars?" The corner of his mouth lifted, drawing all of Clementine's attention to his dimples.

She laughed. "Touché. You've got it all over Rudolph."

One by one, they hooked the dogs up to the sled,

which Ben secured with a heavy anchor device he called the ice hook. Thanks to her sled dog training, Clementine could actually pitch in and help get everything ready. Ben explained they would be using six dogs, which was plenty for recreational mushing. Big teams of sixteen, like the ones in the Gold Rush Trail, were typically only used for racing.

Clementine snapped the neck line to the halter of a pale gray husky in one of the lead dog positions at the very front. The dog would be running double lead, alongside Kodiak.

She wondered where the rest of the dogs came from. Something told her they weren't Ben's, but she decided to cut him some slack and stop asking unnecessary questions. Then again, if she did, maybe he would quiet her with another kiss.

Thankfully, he filled her in without her having to ask. "These guys belong to a friend of mine. Reggie Chase. He's mushing in the race, but these are his second-string dogs."

He ran his hand along the length of the gang line, double-checking every hook and lead along the way. As Clementine followed, her gaze flitted back to the dog yard, empty now that the dogs had been hooked up to the sled. She tried to imagine Ben here alone, looking out over all those cheery red doghouses, vacant and barren. Just the thought of it made her heart hurt. She longed to ask him why he apparently no longer mushed, but she didn't want to ruin the moment.

Later. I'll ask him later.

"You ready to go for a ride?" he asked, and a shiver ran up her spine.

"I am."

"Okay. Hop up here on the sled runners." He helped get her feet situated, one on each runner, and placed her hands about shoulder-width apart on the drive bow.

And suddenly, she was nervous.

She couldn't even remember the command for go. Was it giddyup? No. That worked on horses. Hike. Yes, that was it. Hike.

Oh Lord, what if I get miles away and I panic?

She glanced at Ben over her shoulder. "You're not staying behind are you?"

"No." His jaw clenched, as if the very idea caused him physical pain. Clementine found it oddly comforting.

Then, instead of walking to the front of the sled and situating himself in the basket as she'd expected, he stepped up onto the runners directly behind her. His arms, big and strong, wrapped around her shoulders and he held on to the drive bow with his hands next to hers. Clementine's head tucked neatly against his shoulder.

He bent his head and said in a low voice, "I was planning on riding back here, if that's okay with you."

Something told her this was most definitely not the way Aidan would have taught her how to mush. "It's wonderful, actually. You're like a big, warm blanket."

He chuckled behind her and his breath tickled the back of her neck. "I'm ready when you are. I've already released the ice hook. Just remember to step on the brake if you want to slow down. I'm right here if you need any help."

She tightened her grip on the drive bow, took a deep breath and shouted, "Hike."

The dogs sprang into action as if they'd been waiting their entire lives to hear that one syllable. All barking ceased and their paws scrambled for footing in the deep snow. Clementine let out a little yelp and held on tight as the sled bounced into action.

Then Ben's voice was suddenly in her ear, sounding strong and reassuring. "Don't worry. The ride will get much smoother in a minute."

And he was right. It took a few beats for the dogs to find their rhythm, but before a full sixty seconds passed, they were moving in perfect harmony. Even their tails wagged in unison.

"I'm doing it. I'm really doing it," Clementine called over her shoulder.

"You sure are. This trail makes a big loop through the trees surrounding my property. The dogs should stay put, but you know what to do if they get off track. *Gee* for right and *Haw* for left."

"Got it."

At first, Ben's closeness was somewhat of a distraction. A very *pleasant* distraction. She wasn't sure if she knew up from down, much less a gee from a haw. She worried the dogs would run headfirst into a tree and she wouldn't even notice.

But the more ground they covered, the more she relaxed. Not that she would have been able to do otherwise. The sun dipped below the horizon, bathing the trail in soft hues of purple and blue that took her breath away. The deeper they traveled into the forest, the quieter the world became. She heard nothing but the gentle footfalls of the dogs and the soft swish of the sled moving through the snow. Even though they were moving, she felt as if she was suspended in a moment of perfect stillness. She sank against Ben's chest and thought this was perhaps the most peaceful and enchanting instant of her life.

Thank You, God.

She glanced up at the velvet sky. The stars in Alaska were bigger and brighter than she'd ever seen before. And in this quiet moment, she thought they just might be shining for her and Ben alone.

With her gaze still fixed on the sky, she asked, "Have you ever seen the aurora borealis?"

Her voice was barely above a whisper, but it still felt odd breaking the tranquil silence.

"Yes, many times," he whispered back.

"Is it amazing?"

"Yes. It's interesting that you ask me about that now. Some of the most extravagant auroras I've seen have been out on the trail." He dipped his head, and his breath warmed the crook of her neck. "The darker the night, the brighter they shine."

"The darker the night, the brighter they shine," she repeated. "I like that."

"In the Middle Ages, the auroras were thought to be a sign from God." He released a soft sigh. "Funny. I haven't thought about that in a long time."

"I would love to see Him light up the sky."

"Maybe you will," he murmured.

"I hope so." She burrowed into him and let her gaze linger once again on the starlit night.

As the dogs carried them home with quiet footsteps, Clementine felt as though she were floating high above the canopy of trees. She was weightless, nothing but a breath on the wind. She smiled, closed her eyes, and could have sworn she could feel the diamond dust swirling and dancing against her skin.

Chapter Eight

"You should have been there. It was lovely." Clementine sipped her coffee—today's blend was dark mocha almond—and exhaled a dreamy sigh. She glanced at her companion and waited for an appropriate reaction to her detailed description of her mushing lesson the night before.

Nugget cocked her head, blinked and went back to sniffing the sidewalk.

"I get it." Clementine frowned down at the Pomeranian. "You're more interested in all the exciting smells around here than my love life."

Nugget agreed with a wag of her tail.

Love life. Since when did she have a love life? And why was she entertaining such thoughts when she was on a business trip?

Clementine needed to clear her head. She briefly considered going back to the coffee bar and chatting with Anya, but the barista had been busy mixing one latte after another for a swarm of guests when

Clementine last saw her. So instead, she followed Nugget's zigzag trail down the walkway surrounding the hotel.

She should have been back in her room, typing up notes for the magazine. For once, Clementine found it difficult to even think about work. Her mind was still reeling from the mushing lesson with Ben. Undoubtedly it had been the most romantic night of her life.

And that kiss! Yes, some head-clearing was definitely in order.

Clementine's gaze darted to the few people who were up and out in the frigid weather, strolling in the early morning frost. She was sure she was blushing. No one seemed to notice. Either that or they mistook her flush for windburn.

She pulled the collar of her parka up until it covered most of her face, and suppressed a shiver at the recollection of the evening's events. If she closed her eyes, she could hear the sled runners gliding through the forest. The mushing itself was a revelation. She'd never expected it to be so peaceful, so quiet. She'd jokingly told Ben she wanted to start a Texas dog sled team, as his father had done in Florida. This morning, she'd found a perfectly sized T-shirt for Nugget in the hotel gift shop that said "Sled Dog in Training." So far, it had elicited quite a few laughs from passersby on their morning stroll.

Lost in her thoughts, Clementine almost spilled her coffee when Nugget suddenly ran at full speed to the end of her leash. If she'd weighed more than a few pounds, she would have pulled Clementine's arm out of its socket.

"Nugget, what in the world? The T-shirt is only a joke, you know."

She gave the lead a gentle tug and attempted to reel her in, but was met with rottweiler-sized resistance from the pint-sized dog. Nugget's entire body quivered with excitement and she let forth a series of earsplitting yaps.

When Clementine bent to scoop the unruly dog into her arms, she caught a glimpse of a pair of mismatched eyes peering out at her from ice-covered shrubbery nearby. One blue, one brown, she recognized them instantly as sled dog eyes. She'd never seen any other kind of dog with two different-colored eyes before.

"Hi, buddy," she cooed.

The eyes stared back at her with cool indifference while Nugget attempted to wiggle out from Clementine's grasp. As anxious as the Pomeranian was to meet the strange dog, the feeling evidently wasn't mutual.

"Nugget, I'm afraid you're not helping matters." Clementine straightened, backed away a few feet and waited.

After her cup of coffee was halfway drained, it became clear that the husky had no intention of revealing itself so long as Nugget was present. Clementine hoped it was an extreme case of shyness, but couldn't help but worry that the dog was injured or in some kind of distress.

She crouched down to make sure it hadn't gotten away, although that would have been impossible because she'd been standing guard outside the shrubbery since the moment she'd spotted it. At first glance, she didn't see anything but a tangle of branches and twigs dripping with icicles. She frowned. Once she finally spotted the husky eyes, set above a trembling black nose, her lips curved up with relief. The dog had moved even deeper into the hedge.

"Don't go anywhere," Clementine urged. "I'll be right back with a treat."

She wasted no time getting Nugget settled in the hotel room. The Pomeranian watched her every move as she shoved handfuls of dog biscuits into her pockets. Nugget shimmied to the very edge of the bed and wagged her tail, fully expecting to be showered with the treats. Clementine gave her a kiss on the head and a ridiculously oversized rawhide chew she'd been saving for the plane ride home, and managed to escape the room still armed with the dog biscuits.

To her great relief she found the husky right where she'd left it, cowering in the bushes. Clementine knelt on the ground, a sacrifice she hoped the dog appreciated considering the sidewalk was covered in ice.

Palm up, she held out a biscuit. "Are you hungry?"

The black nose twitched and moved an inch or two closer.

"Yum, yum." She tossed the treat into the bushes and was rewarded with the immediate sound of crunching.

"Want another one?"

By the fourth biscuit, Clementine had a happy, wagging Alaskan husky in her lap. A quick inspection told her the dog was a girl, and sadly, had no collar.

"What are we going to do with you, huh?"

Ben was working at the paper until evening and Clementine didn't know where she could find the closest veterinary office or animal shelter. She looped her crocheted winter scarf around the husky's neck as a makeshift leash. She sent up a silent prayer of thanks that the dog seemed timid and controllable, and led her inside the hotel lobby.

Anya looked up from behind the coffee counter. Her eyebrows nearly shot to her hairline. "You got another dog?"

"I just found her outside. She doesn't have a collar." Clementine ran a protective hand over the dog's pointy ears. The husky gazed up at her. "She seems to be a sweetheart."

"I can see it now. You're going to take that dog home to Texas, aren't you?" She laughed and clicked a lever on the espresso machine.

It sounded like something Ben would say. Clementine didn't want to admit that the notion had in-

deed crossed her mind. Not that she would actually
go through with it, would she? "I need to get her to
a shelter or veterinary clinic. Somewhere that has
a microchip scanner. I'm sure she belongs to someone. She looks like a sled dog."

"The Humane Society is six blocks that way."
Anya tipped her head in the direction of where
Clementine's dog handling classes had been held.

"Great. Thanks."

Clementine was a tad wary about walking a
strange dog six blocks with nothing more than a
knit scarf for a leash, but she had no choice. Nugget's tiny collar would barely qualify as an ankle
bracelet on the husky. The gift shop, while chock-
full of the Sled Dog in Training T-shirts and moose-
shaped dog toys, had nothing practical to offer. So
off they went.

The dog moved at an easy lope next to Clementine. She panted softly, with her mouth open in a
way that made it look as though she were smiling.
Clementine stopped and fed her a biscuit every block
or so. She liked to think of it as positive reinforce-
ment for staying close by, rather than a bribe. Either
way, it worked. The husky was still trotting happily
beside her as they approached the block with the
Humane Society.

The receptionist glanced at the dog when they
walked in. "Looks like a husky."

Clementine wasn't sure what she'd expected when
she first entered the humane society, but she couldn't

help feeling let down by the receptionist's casual re-action. Was finding a stray sled dog really so com-monplace?

Clementine nodded. "I found her in front of the Northern Lights Inn. She probably belongs to some-one. I was hoping you could check to see if she's microchipped."

"I'll need to take her around back." The woman came out from behind the counter and slid a slip lead around the dog's neck in place of the scarf.

The husky's mismatched eyes swiveled to Clem-entine with a pleading expression.

Clementine handed the receptionist a dog biscuit. "Here. She likes these."

The two of them disappeared behind a closed door. Clementine wound her scarf back around her neck. It smelled like dog. She removed it and shoved it in the pocket of her parka, on top of the crumbs from all the biscuits.

She's a beautiful dog. I'm sure she belongs to someone. They'll get her owner's information from the microchip and she'll be home in no time.

Maybe she even belonged to one of the mushers from the race and had somehow gotten lost. Clem-entine put forth great effort to picture her running across the frozen tundra of interior Alaska in front of a sled. But every time she tried, the only sled she could conjure up in her imagination was Ben's. Once again she felt the warmth of Ben's breath on the back of her neck, his arms around her, reaching for the drive bow.

Her stomach fluttered.

She took a deep, steadying breath and wandered around the lobby. On the wall adjacent to the front desk, there was a large bulletin board with photos of pets up for adoption. Clementine was stunned to find at least a dozen dogs that resembled huskies looking back at her from the pictures of adoptable dogs. The delightful flutter in her belly changed quickly into a sinking feeling.

"Ma'am?" The receptionist walked back in with the lost dog.

To her dismay, Clementine knew the moment she saw the look on the woman's face that the news was not good. Even more to her dismay, the dog wagged her tail and bounded toward Clementine.

"There was no microchip, was there?"

"I'm afraid not." The receptionist positioned herself back behind the counter and sighed. "I suppose you'd like to surrender the dog to our care."

A guilty knot lodged in Clementine's throat. She could barely speak around it. "Hmm…" She looked down at the dog. Huge mistake.

"Well?" The receptionist drummed her fingernails on the desk.

"Um, how many Alaskan huskies do you already have here up for adoption?" Clementine gestured toward the bulletin board, careful not to catch the dog's gaze again. Although a tiny voice in her head told her it was too late.

"At least ten." This was accompanied by a nonchalant shrug. "We get them all the time."

"I'm surprised. Do any of the mushers ever adopt them?"

"A few. Most of them breed their own dogs. There was this one guy who used to have an all-rescue team. He doesn't race anymore."

Clementine wondered if she was talking about Ben. Surely not. He'd said he mushed but didn't mention anything about racing. Clementine looked back down at the dog, stalling for time.

The fingernail drumming resumed, and the receptionist lifted a curious brow. "So what would you like to do with the dog?"

Clementine gulped.

Lord, help me out here.

Ben was late.

He'd risen early and managed to return Reggie's dogs in plenty of time to get to the paper by nine o'clock. Everything was running according to schedule until a big obstacle got in his way. A certain big, *furry* obstacle.

"Quit being so stubborn." Ben cross his arms and glared at Kodiak. "Get in the car."

The husky yawned dramatically, but otherwise didn't move a muscle. He remained perched on top of the red doghouse, sitting ramrod straight. Snow

had already begun to accumulate on his coat in a
fine layer, changing his appearance from charcoal to
almost silver. He stared back at Ben unflinchingly.

"I'm already late for work. We've got to go. I'm
serious. Get. In. The. Car."

He waited a full minute. Kodiak didn't budge.
Ben wasn't altogether sure he even blinked. He'd
become a statue.

"Fine. I'm going." Ben turned his back to the dog
and waved over his shoulder.

It was a bluff, of course. Nothing but a ruse to
tempt Kodiak into bounding willingly into the car.
Ben was scheduled to spend four more nights at the
hotel before heading to Nome for the end of the race.
He wasn't about to leave Kodiak behind.

He left the passenger door wide open, an invitation, and climbed in the driver's seat. He started
the car and forced himself to look away from the
dog yard before Kodiak got a glimpse of the smile
creeping its way to his lips.

Frigid air blasted from the vents on his already-
frozen hands. He was late for work. His faithful dog
had suddenly developed a nasty rebellious streak.
Yet, Ben still smiled.

He'd kissed Clementine. And she'd kissed him
back.

Nothing else mattered.

At the time, he'd meant to shock her into silence.
At least that's what he wanted to believe. But something happened when their lips met.

With that one kiss, Ben felt more complete, more whole than he had since the accident. Clementine claimed to see stars. Ben felt them, rising up in his soul, filling him with hope. More hope than he'd known in years.

He wasn't sure what it meant. Clementine didn't belong to him. She didn't even live in Alaska. And if she did, the energy required to keep her safe and sound would send him to an early grave.

But for those precious moments when he'd held her in his arms, Ben could feel the ice around his heart melting. Thawing, ever so slowly.

He turned back to the window, no longer caring if Kodiak saw the look on his face. The dog was smart. Ben would never be able to hide the kind of bone-deep contentment he felt. Or the occasional thrill that coursed through him when he remembered the feel of Clementine in his arms. Soft, sweet, womanly.

It was really a shame he had to go into work when all he wanted to do was get back to the Northern Lights Inn. But the sooner he got to the office, the sooner he'd be finished.

He fixed his gaze on Kodiak and assessed the situation. Clearly the dog had no intention of coming down. At least not by choice.

Ben got out of the car and strode back to the yard. He could tell Kodiak was pretending not to watch his approach, but the subtle twitch of his whiskers gave him away.

This time, Ben walked all the way to his dog-house and gave the husky a good rub between the ears. "Come on, buddy, what's the matter?"

Kodiak let out a mournful whine and leaned against Ben.

And suddenly he understood.

He wrapped his arm around Kodiak's neck. "You had fun last night, huh, bud?"

A series of *woo-woos* followed.

"I know it's been a long time. You've missed it." He stopped short of admitting he'd missed mushing, too. "But that's not our life anymore."

The dog grew silent. He didn't need to say anything for Ben to get the message loud and clear. First Reggie, then Clementine, now his dog. And even though he never pushed, Ben's father. Was there anyone out there who *didn't* think he should be mushing again?

Ben glanced at the sky.

I suppose You have an opinion on the matter, too?

It was a cloudless morning. Bright and clear, without so much as a snowflake in the sky. Eerily similar to the last time Ben had fixed his gaze on heaven in search of an answer.

But even now, no direct answer came. There was no need. The difference this time was that Ben sensed God speaking to his heart daily. It was a strange sensation that had begun when Clementine had come into his life. Sometimes Ben wondered if He'd been there all along. He wanted to believe that was the case, and he'd simply been too wounded to notice. But he wasn't quite ready to accept it.

He turned his attention back to what he knew to be true. Something concrete.

"Kodiak, we've got to go. Come on." He ruffled the fur on the husky's shoulders and headed back toward the car.

This time the dog followed quickly on his heels. Ben didn't need to turn around to make sure he was there. He simply knew.

Clementine was unprepared for the sight of Ben sitting at the coffee bar when she finally returned to the Northern Lights Inn. Even after walking an extra five blocks or so to pick up a proper-sized leash and collar for the stray, she thought she would have plenty of time to put some sort of plan in place.

And a plan was definitely in order.

Keeping the dog had seemed like a great idea at the time. If she'd left the husky at the shelter, she would have been just one of a dozen other similar dogs waiting to be adopted. On the other hand, Ben was a musher without a team. And he had all those cute little doghouses, sitting empty next to his cabin.

She'd convinced herself he would be thrilled. After all, Ben loved Kodiak. Still, there was a niggle somewhere in her consciousness that told her she was overstepping her bounds. The niggle grew stronger as the hotel came into view. By the time Ben swiveled on his bar stool and his confused gaze swept over the stray dog, the niggle practically clobbered Clementine over the head.

She breathed in a sigh of relief when he rose to greet her. "Hey, you."

He smiled, and Clementine felt as though she were drowning in diamond dust. "Hey."

She almost forgot about the dog on the end of her leash until Kodiak rose to touch noses with her. The two huskies wagged their plumed tails in unison.

"What happened to Nugget? She's grown." Ben patted the bar stool next to him. A large coffee cup sat in front of it, overflowing with whipped cream and sprinkles.

Sprinkles. How sweet.

A guilty knot formed in Clementine's stomach. "This isn't Nugget, silly."

"I gathered." He gave the stray a suspicious once-over. "So who's your friend?"

From behind the bar, Anya waved and flipped the little sign on the register to the side that said On Break. She gave Clementine a grim smile before slinging a dishrag over her shoulder and disappearing.

Clementine wished she would have stayed. She could use a little backup right about now. "I found her."

"Really? Where?"

"Right out front." Clementine nodded toward the revolving doors. "She was cowering in the bushes."

"Poor thing. The Humane Society isn't far from

here. I'll walk her over there with you and we can have her scanned for a microchip."

Clementine inhaled a steadying breath. "I've already been there."

Ben frowned, and the first lines of worry creased his brow. "What did they say?"

"No microchip." It was now or never. Clementine took a sip of her coffee. It was hot, too hot, but she barely noticed. "There were so many dogs there, Ben. All homeless. I couldn't leave her there."

"What exactly are you planning on doing with her?" There was a panicked edge to his voice. He sounded similar to the way he had when he'd stormed into her dog handling class, convinced she'd been hurt.

"Texas is awfully warm for a sled dog," she murmured.

Ben's jaw twitched and his eyes grew dark, stormy. Clearly they both knew she wasn't planning on taking the dog home.

Kodiak and the stray chose that moment to curl into two identical balls on the floor, right next to one another. They looked like two peas—albeit furry ones—in a pod.

Their apparent acceptance of one another bolstered her confidence. "Look, they like each other. That's great because I was thinking you could take her."

Ben shook his head. "No."

Clementine ignored him and made a case for the

poor dog. "She's all alone in the world, and you have all that room at your place. Look at her. I'll bet she'd make a great sled dog."

He turned sharp eyes on her. "I don't need a sled dog."

"You sort of do."

"I most definitely do *not,*" he said through clenched teeth.

The rich scent of freshly ground coffee beans, combined with something else—chocolate, maybe— filled the air. What would have ordinarily smelled delicious suddenly seemed sickeningly sweet. Combined with the rising tide of worry in the pit of Clementine's stomach, it was enough to make her push the coffee a few inches away.

He had to take the dog. What else would Clementine do with her?

She swiveled on her bar stool and leveled her gaze at him. "Are you the same man who took me mushing last night?"

The stubborn set of his jaw softened somewhat. "That was a one-time thing."

Clementine's heart clenched. She couldn't help but wonder if the kiss had also been a one-time thing. The kiss, the diamond dust, everything. She was beginning to feel like Cinderella with her lost slipper. The magic of the night before had vanished and was replaced by this harsh reality. Wasn't that always the way with romance? In Clementine's experience, most definitely. "Why?"

"Because I don't mush anymore." He stared into his untouched coffee. The whipped cream had begun to melt and drip down the sides of his cup. "Period."

"You did last night."

"That was last night. This is today." He pushed away from the coffee bar, nearly knocking his bar stool over.

Taking his cue, the two dogs rose. Kodiak nudged Ben's leg with a poke of his nose. The stray did the same. Ben backed away as if he'd been electrocuted. "I can't do this."

Clementine laid a protective hand on the dog's head. "Can't or won't?"

"Both." He shoved his arms into his parka and crammed his hands into its pockets.

"Ben, please." Clementine felt like begging, although she was unsure what exactly she was begging for. The conversation had taken a dangerous turn.

"Clementine." He held up a hand to stop her. "Don't."

The sight of that hand—signaling to her as if she were a dog herself, trained to do his bidding—sparked something in Clementine. She no longer felt guilty for trying to impose the dog on him. In fact, she wouldn't have let him take the dog now if her life depended on it. "Don't what?"

He dropped his hand and, with it, his defenses dropped as well. The anger disappeared from his features, leaving nothing but raw pain etched there for all the world to see.

It hurt Clementine's heart to look at him, but a team of world-class sled dogs wouldn't have the strength to make her look anywhere else.

"Just...don't." He pulled his hood down low over his eyes, turned and walked through the revolving lobby doors with Kodiak trailing on his heels.

Clementine, left with the distinct impression he was no longer talking about dogs or mushing at all, could do nothing but watch him walk away.

Chapter Nine

"What just happened?" Clementine muttered to herself as she watched Ben and Kodiak disappear into a swirl of snow in the parking lot.

"Come sit down," Anya called from behind her. "I'll refresh your coffee."

Clementine hadn't even realized the barista had returned. She'd been too wrapped up in what was happening with Ben—or not happening, as it were. And now, on top of everything, she had a stray husky still on her hands.

She slumped on one of the bar stools at the coffee bar. Her drink still sat there, its tower of whipped cream having long melted into a pool on the counter. Bright streaks of color were the only thing left of the sprinkles. "I'm sorry about the mess, Anya."

"Don't worry about it. I've seen worse, believe me." Anya took the cup, along with Ben's, and wiped away the puddles with a swipe of her dishrag.

If only the mess Clementine had made of everything with Ben could be wiped away just as easily. She sighed and looked down at the stray dog, who sat with her chin on Clementine's thigh.

She rested her hand on the husky's head. "I'm sorry, girl. I gave it a try."

"Not to be nosy, but did you just ask Ben to give this sweetie here a home?" Anya set a fresh cup of coffee on the counter and pushed it toward Clementine.

"You're not being nosy. It's not like it was a secret. I asked him right here." She sighed and took a sip from the cup Anya offered her. "Thanks for this. It's delicious."

Anya shrugged. "You looked like you could use it. Plus a friend. I could help out with both, if you like."

"That would be really nice." Clementine smiled. It would be nice to have a girlfriend in Aurora, even if she was there only temporarily.

Anya poured herself a small cup of coffee from the pot labeled Decaf. She gave Clementine's latte a look filled with yearning. "Yours looks infinitely yummier, but I shouldn't drink those things all day long. I try to resist the temptation."

"One of the hazards of the job, I guess." Clementine guiltily gazed at her tower of whipped cream and decided Anya must have tremendous willpower.

"Exactly." She took a sip of her cup of plain black decaf and winced. "It's just not the same, I'm afraid."

"So have you lived in Aurora long?" Clementine figured Anya was an Alaska native because her grandmother came from an Inuit family, but didn't know much else.

"Born and raised." Anya nodded. "But I finally moved out of my mom's house a few years ago. I live in an apartment out back."

"Here? At the hotel?"

"Yes. There are a few apartments on the rear of the property, out by the lake, for staff members and long-term renters." Her violet eyes narrowed, but thankfully her smile remained intact. "Wait a minute. Now you're going to try and pawn that dog off on me, aren't you?"

"The thought might have crossed my mind." Clementine bit her lip. She would have been lying if she said the idea hadn't occurred to her.

"Sorry." Anya shook her head. "I wish I could help out, but I already have a dog. At least I think I do."

"You think you do?"

"He's a rescue dog. He's shy." Anya sighed. "Actually, that's a bit of an understatement. I haven't seen him for a couple of days. He likes to hide under the bed. I think someone mistreated him in the past. It's painful to watch."

"Oh." Clementine had thought her heart couldn't sink any lower, but she'd been wrong.

Guilt pricked her conscience as she took in Anya's worried expression. Obviously she had her own share of problems to deal with.

She reached for Anya's hand and gave it a sympathetic squeeze. "I'm sorry about your dog. I'll bet if you give it time, he'll come around."

"That's what I'm hoping." The barista shifted her gaze toward the stray. "Do you think she'd like some water?"

"She might. We've had quite the adventure this afternoon. We walked all over Aurora."

"I'll get some for her." Anya glanced around the lobby—checking around for customers, Clementine presumed—before disappearing behind a slick wooden door labeled Employees Only.

She returned a few moments later with a large bowl of water and a tiny white bag.

"What's this?" Clementine asked as Anya dropped the bag on the counter.

"A doggy bag, of course." Anya winked. "I grabbed a few bites of tenderloin from the restaurant kitchen. The poor girl is homeless. I figured she could use a special treat."

"Thank you." Clementine tucked the bag in her purse. She'd mix the steak with dog food for the next few meals.

The next few meals.

Her stomach lurched. How long would she have this dog? And what would she do if she hadn't found her a home before it was time to go back to Texas?

As if she could read her thoughts, Anya cleared her throat and whispered, "What do you think you'll do with her?"

The way she lowered her voice when she asked the question, as if the dog might overhear, touched Clementine. Yes, she could definitely see herself becoming fast friends with Anya.

"I honestly don't know." Clementine took another sip of her latte and tried not to look at the stray. She was afraid she might cry if she did. "I really thought Ben would want her. Or that he'd at least think about it."

Anya scrubbed an invisible spot on the counter with her dishrag. "You and Ben seem to be getting close."

Clementine gave a tiny nod. She'd thought they were, especially after he'd kissed her. Now she wasn't so sure.

Why am I so disappointed? I'm not looking for love. Or a relationship. And even if I were, it wouldn't be with someone who lives across the world.

Would it?

"Go easy on him." Anya's eyes grew serious. "He's been through…a lot. I haven't seen him get close to anyone for years."

Her words had the effect of both worrying Clementine and reassuring her all at the same time. She wondered what exactly Anya meant when she'd said Ben had gone through a lot. Whatever it was, she knew it must have something to do with why he no longer mushed.

She closed her eyes and all those sad, empty dog-

houses flashed in her memory. They brought a pang
to her heart, and she let her eyes flutter open once
more.

Of one thing, she was certain—whatever Anya
knew about Ben's past would remain a secret until
he told her the story himself. She had a feeling that if
Anya knew about it, everyone else in Aurora did as
well. Alaska might be the biggest state in the country, but Aurora was still a small town. Clementine
had been upset when Ben refused to take the stray,
but she wasn't about to betray his trust by digging
into his past hurts behind his back.

She gave Anya a smile. It was a weary one, but
the best she could muster under the circumstances.

Anya gathered their empty coffee cups and offered a few more words of reassurance. "He'll come
around. It's like with my dog. He needs time. That's
all."

Clementine watched as she turned toward the sink
and plunged the cups in soapy water. She wished she
could take Anya's encouragement to heart, but the
one thing she and Ben didn't have was time.

In the dim glow of the morning sunrise, Ben
paced a worn trail in front of the Northern Lights
Inn. Sometime during the night, the temperature
had dropped close to zero. About an hour ago, he'd
ventured a look at himself in the reflection of the
glass doors and noticed his beard glittering, filled
with ice crystals. He couldn't remember the last time

he'd stayed outside in the cold long enough for that to happen.

Yet here he was, pacing in the snow.

It had begun as a penance. Any man fool enough to kiss a woman until she saw stars and then turn around and disappoint her so bitterly deserved to suffer. Or so Ben had thought as he lay sleepless in his hotel bed.

He'd been so convinced she was the one in the wrong. How could she ask him to take the dog after what he'd been through? Then, as he'd asked the question aloud—to God, he presumed—it had hit him with startling clarity.

Clementine didn't know what he'd been through.

How could she possibly know that when Ben looked into the eyes of that stray, he saw the eyes of all the dogs he'd loved and lost?

It was his fault, of course. He'd never told her about the accident. He'd been all too ready to believe the omission was because he didn't talk about his past. To anyone. But in the dead of night he'd come to the realization that he hadn't told her because he didn't want her to look at him like everyone else did. To the rest of the mushing world, he was a disappointment. He couldn't disappoint Clementine if she never knew he was once on the cusp of greatness.

But it was too late. The look in her eyes when he'd walked away from her spoke volumes. He'd disappointed her plenty.

Would it have killed him to take the dog?

Maybe.

Probably not.

The very idea wove a knot of anxiety in his gut. But that would pass, wouldn't it?

He wasn't sure. The only thing he knew without a doubt was that he needed to explain himself to Clementine. He owed her that much.

The moment he reached that decision was the instant his penance had turned into a vigil. Sleep had eluded him thus far. He might as well stay outside until Clementine brought Nugget out for her morning walk. And the stray, if she had taken up residence in Clementine's room. Ben would bet his life that she had. Clementine would probably mush that dog all the way back to Texas before she'd turn her in to the animal shelter. That's the kind of person she was. Caring. Compassionate. Beneath all of her carefree spontaneity and quest for independence, she was a marshmallow.

The marshmallow was getting to him.

He should have known he was treading on thin ice when he'd agreed to take her mushing. Deep down, he knew she would have been fine learning how to mush with Aidan. Most likely. But most likely wasn't good enough where Clementine was concerned. If she was going to mush, he'd wanted to be the one to teach her. He'd wanted to see the delight on her face when she felt that first swish through the snow. And she had lit up, almost as much as when he'd kissed her.

Then he'd gone and ruined everything by running like a frightened rabbit at the sight of that stray dog.

Perfect love casts out fear.

He'd looked up the verse in the Bible back in his room after Clementine had first quoted it to him. He let the words soothe him. Concentrating on them stopped the shaking of his hands, still cold despite the hand warmers in his pockets.

Calmed, at least for the moment, Ben decided to put his restless energy to good use and do something nice for Clementine. Perhaps if he could put a smile on her face, she'd be more likely to listen to the explanation of his disappearing act. Armed with little more than snow, he didn't have many options. Flowers would have been near impossible to find in Aurora in the dead of winter, even if he did want to leave and risk the chance of missing her when she emerged from the hotel. A risk he most definitely did not want to take.

So he went to work, constructing the perfectly proportioned snowman.

His effort earned more than a few snickers from passersby. Alaskans lived with snow nine months out of the year, so for most of them, snowmen had lost their novelty. He looked like a tourist. Fortunately, the number of amused witnesses was few in the predawn hours. Just as he finished shaping the head and adding two almost evenly sized stick arms, Clementine spun out of the revolving door.

He knew it was her without even having to turn

to look, as if he could sense her presence. When he did turn, it was as if the sun had been waiting to rise until she appeared. Gentle rays of morning sunshine caressed her cheeks, giving her a warm, cozy glow. No amount of diamond dust could have made her more beautiful in Ben's eyes.

He swallowed, with great difficulty.

Just as he'd suspected, she was flanked on either side by dogs. Tiny Nugget scurried alongside her right, and the stray stuck like glue to her left. Neither were tethered with leashes, but like planets circling the sun, they stayed in her orbit. Ben felt the pull himself and was powerless against it.

She spotted him before he could say anything. The smile that was her constant accessory dimmed at first until she noticed his frozen companion. As her gaze swept the giant snowman—its size was impressive, even for Alaska—she let out a little laugh. Her steps slowed, but she walked toward him, accompanied by her canine entourage.

Ben forced himself to look at Nugget and the sled dog and include them both in his greeting. "Good morning."

"Good morning. Who's your friend?" The fact that she echoed the question he'd asked when he'd first seen the stray wasn't lost on Ben.

"This guy?" Ben nodded toward the snowman. "I suppose you could consider him a peace offering."

"For me?" Her eyes danced, and Ben's heart danced along with them.

"Yes, for you," he answered, loving that she found such pleasure in something as simple as a snowman. "Do you like it?"

"Very much." She grinned and inspected the snowman from all angles. "So he's a peace offering?"

Ben nodded, his throat growing dry with apprehension. But he plowed on. "Yes. I'm sorry about yesterday."

"Don't apologize. It's fine, really." Her lovely lips turned down in the corners, and Ben wanted to tell her no, everything was not fine. How could it be when he'd made her sad?

"Walk with me?" He held out his hand and hoped against hope she would take it.

She did.

Ben's hand was freezing. It felt inhumanely cold, so Clementine clasped it with both of hers, hoping to warm it. His beard was even coated with a fine layer of frost. He looked wilder than she'd ever seen him, like the musher he'd once been.

As if privy to her thoughts, he whispered, "I want to explain why I don't mush anymore."

"Okay." She bit her lip, suddenly afraid of whatever he was going to say.

She knew with certainty that this was it. He was going to tell her the secret that Anya and everyone else in Aurora already knew. Ben Grayson was a man of few words. The snowman towering beside them only underscored the importance of the moment. If Ben wanted to explain himself, she was more than willing to listen.

Ben pulled her alongside him and led her to the small path that trailed around to the back of the hotel. Kodiak uncurled himself from the tight ball where he'd half buried himself in the snow and quickly caught up with the other two dogs. They all moved in silence until they reached the frozen lake.

Clementine had never ventured back here before, and she found it like another world. The white, barren patch of lake stretched out almost as far as she could see. Where it stopped, tall pine trees stood guard, as if separating this quiet, private space from the rest of existence.

The dogs scampered into the fresh snow, yipping and barking. The echo of their voices bouncing off the trees broke the silence. Clementine was aware of only one other sound—Ben, breathing steadily beside her.

Finally he spoke. "I mushed the Gold Rush Trail for the first time eight years ago. It was my dad's final year in the race. He finished in the top five as usual, and I came in at number twenty."

Clementine nodded. Finishing the race at all as a rookie was an impressive feat. Placing in the top twenty the first time out was almost unheard of. When Ben told her he knew how to mush, he'd never mentioned he'd been a professional. Yet on some level, she must have known because she wasn't a bit surprised by this revelation.

"By my fourth year, I was a contender. Everyone expected me to win, or at least place in the top three." He shrugged. "The funny thing is, I couldn't have cared less where I ended up. I loved the race. Being out in the open, enjoying the company of my dogs was all I cared about."

His voice broke, sending a spasm of worry straight to Clementine's chest. She squeezed his hand and he continued.

"We were crossing the Bering Sea, heading into Nome. The worst of the trail was behind us—the burn, Dalzell Gorge, Rainy Pass. It should have been a clear shot to the finish. The sun was shining and the sky was clear. There were a few snow flurries, but visibility was good. In fact, it was a day quite like this one." He shook his head, as if he still couldn't believe what happened next. "It caught me so off guard. I had no idea."

Clementine waited for Ben to continue, but instead he grew quiet and kept his gaze fixed on the distance. He stared out across the frozen water until Clementine prompted him. "What happened?"

He cleared his throat, blinked and tore himself away from his memories of the past. Painful memories, to be sure. With each passing minute of silence, Clementine grew more fearful of what she was about to hear.

"It wasn't my first time on the Bering Sea and at

first, this one was no different. Then I heard it, an unmistakable crack that made my heart stop." Ben's free hand flew to his chest, clutching the ache that clearly had never gone away.

Clementine wished she knew how to comfort him. She kept holding his free hand, hoping it provided some sort of reassurance.

"I watched my team, all sixteen dogs, disappear under the ice. One by one."

Before she could stop herself, Clementine gasped. She couldn't imagine witnessing something so awful. Just the thought of it made her want to squeeze her eyes shut tight. But she forced them to stay open and meet Ben's gaze.

His blue eyes were etched with equal parts pain and weariness. "I threw the ice hook and the sled stopped. The hole in the ice was small—no bigger than the width of a pair of dogs. But they were all attached to the gang line, so they followed one another into the sea. I tried everything I could to get them out. I was up to my shoulders in half-frozen water when the next musher on the trail found me, frostbit and in shock."

"Just you?" She hated to ask the question but needed to know the answer.

"Me and Kodiak. He was the only one I managed to save." Ben's gaze locked on to the husky, romping through the fresh snow with the other two dogs. Ben's masculine features seemed to soften whenever he looked at Kodiak.

No wonder the two of them share such a bond, Clementine thought.

She swallowed around the lump lodged in her throat. "And the others?"

"Gone." He shook his head slowly, thoughtfully. "All fifteen of them. They were my team, my family, and I let them down."

"No," Clementine protested. "It was an accident."

He didn't argue with her, but the stubborn set of his jaw told her he would never believe it was something as simple as an accident.

The mystery of Ben Grayson became crystal clear at once. Everything Clementine knew about him, from his overprotective streak to his unexplained anger toward God, could be traced back to one moment in time. What happened on the Bering Sea had birthed the man that stood next to her. The man he'd been before had vanished along with his dog team. And even though she'd never known that man, Clementine found herself blinking back tears of grief for his loss.

"Ben, I had no idea." Her voice was little more than a hoarse whisper. "I'm so sorry."

"Don't apologize." He shook his head and gave her a weak attempt at a smile. "I took you mushing because I wanted to do it. And I enjoyed every minute of it."

Clementine bit her lip, unsure what to say next.

"But that doesn't mean I'm going to return to that life." Ben glanced at the stray husky. For the first time, he really seemed to look directly at her. "And I don't know if I can take that dog. I want to do it...for you. I just don't know if I can. All of my dogs were rescues. They started as strays, just like this one."

"It's okay." She fought the tears that wanted to stream down her cheeks. "Really."

"Don't take her back to the shelter yet. Give me some time. Can you do that?" He lifted her hand and covered it with a gentle touch of his lips.

"Yes, I can do that." He'd asked for time, just what Anya said he needed. Yet Clementine knew that was the one thing she couldn't give him. Time. She was due to fly back to Texas as soon as the race got under way. But what else could she say?

Ben withdrew a small packet from his pocket and tossed it from one palm to another.

"Hand warmers," he said with a sad smile.

"How bad was the frostbite?" Clementine asked.

"Bad. I was hospitalized for six days and nearly lost my fingers." He didn't have to tell her that he would have gladly traded his fingers for the lives of his dogs. It was written all over his face.

"Do your hands prevent you from mushing competitively again? Would it be possible? If you ever changed your mind, I mean."

An angry vein in his temple throbbed. "My hands aren't the problem."

"You don't miss it? Not at all?" She knew it wasn't what he wanted to hear, and it wasn't any of her business. But she'd seen the way he'd come to life riding on that sled. He belonged on the sled runners.

Irritation flashed in his gaze, but his temper remained in check. "Until I took you out, no. No, I didn't."

"But now you might?" She smiled and made an attempt to lighten the somber mood. "Ben, I know what it's like to go through life not really living. I don't want you to end up with regrets one day. Then you might end up on the back of a motorcycle. With flames."

"With flames?" he cringed. "Never."

Clementine laughed and was instantly grateful when Ben did, too. Their laughter echoed off the pine trees, commingling so that Clementine was unsure where hers left off and Ben's began.

"Can I ask you something?" he said once they'd grown quiet again.

She answered with mock solemnity. "No, I'm not a fan of any type of vehicle with flames. Even sleds."

"Even sleds, huh?"

"Even sleds."

"Then it's a good thing my question has nothing to do with flames." His gaze softened in a way that made Clementine's heart flutter. "How would you feel about going on a proper date with me, Clementine?"

She knew she had no business saying yes. She was scheduled to return home in less than a week. There was an expiration date on whatever friendship they developed, and it was fast approaching. But today, Ben had opened up to her in a way that changed things. She was beginning to doubt whether she would be able to spend more time with him and simply walk away when her trip was over.

Every instinct she possessed told her to say no. She needed to end this now, while she still could. *If* she still could.

"A proper date?" She tried to steady her wobbly voice. "What exactly does that mean?"

"Dinner. Music. No dogs." He took her hand in his. "May I escort you to the Gold Rush Trail Banquet tomorrow night? It's not too fancy…we're still in Alaska. But there will be dinner and a band. We can dress up a bit. I think you might enjoy yourself."

Clementine was fooling herself if she thought she could turn him down. She wasn't sure what she was doing anymore. She wasn't sure of much at all, except that Ben trusted her enough to open up about his past. That, and he wanted to take her out on a date.

And she wanted very much to say yes.

She smiled and pretended they had all the time in the world. "That sounds lovely, Ben."

Chapter Ten

"A date, huh?" Anya topped Clementine's mug with a generous dollop of whipped cream and grinned.

The morning sun streamed in through the window behind her, where Clementine could see the snow-covered lake shimmering with icy crystals.

Beautiful, she mused. But it didn't hold a candle to diamond dust.

"Yes." Clementine nodded absently, as she tried to drag her mind to more practical matters. "A proper date, according to Ben."

"Ben hasn't dated anyone for a long time. Not that I know of anyway. This is exciting." The barista tilted her head. "It is exciting, right? For you, too, I mean."

Clementine reached for her morning coffee and tried to ignore the nagging sense of doubt that had taken up residence in her conscience overnight. "Of course."

Anya eyed her with obvious concern. "Not that

it's any of my business, but you don't exactly look excited."

Clementine's insides swirled. She felt vaguely dizzy. She supposed that's what happened when there were two very different emotions warring with one another inside her head. She lowered her voice and leaned across the counter. "What am I doing, Anya? I can't start dating Ben."

As appealing as it was, it just wasn't conceivable. In the dead of night, when she'd had trouble sleeping, it had seemed downright crazy.

Anya frowned. "Why not? I know you two are attracted to each other. Anyone who's been around the two of you together can see that."

If only it were that simple. Clementine sighed. "I live on the complete opposite side of the country, for one thing."

"There's that." Anya shrugged.

"That's kind of a big deal, don't you think?"

"Not really." She poured two cups of plain, black coffee and handed them to a pair of bearded, burly men at the opposite end of the counter. They were both wearing overalls that looked even thicker and warmer than their parkas. Mushers, no doubt.

"Not really? Are you serious?" Clementine raised a dubious eyebrow.

"Things like distance seem to sort themselves out, don't they? Love conquers all and the like."

Anya poured herself a glass of water, took a sip and grinned.

Clementine plunked her coffee cup down on the counter.

"No one said anything about love," she said, with a bit too much insistence. "Ben asked me on a date. A simple date. It wasn't a marriage proposal or anything."

If marriage was what she wanted, she'd be sitting in her cubicle back in Texas with Mark's ring on her finger. Although on some level, she knew this wasn't a fair comparison. She didn't harbor the same ordinary, sisterly affection for Ben that she had for Mark. Far from it. Whatever she was feeling, it was far from ordinary.

What am I thinking? This is insane.

"No one said anything about love," she repeated, more for her own sake than Anya's.

"Exactly. You're getting ahead of yourself. It's a date. You'll have fun." Anya reached for Clementine's cup. "I'm hereby revoking your caffeine privileges. You need to relax."

"You're right." Clementine nodded, grateful that Anya was there to talk to. If she'd stayed in her room this morning, her stomach would be even more tied up in knots than it already was.

Anya handed her a glass of water the same size as her own. "Besides, there's a much more important thing you need to be worried about."

Clementine sat up a little straighter on her bar stool, grateful to have something to think about other than whatever was happening between her and Ben. "What?"

Anya grinned. "What are you wearing on this date?"

Clementine blinked. With all the tossing and turning she'd done the night before, this was one worry her mind hadn't seized upon. "I have no idea."

Anya turned the sign on the register over to the side that said Closed. "We're going shopping."

Clementine looked at the sign and laughed. "You're just going to close up and take me shopping?"

"I'll take my lunch early." She ducked behind the counter for a moment and popped back up with her purse in tow. "It's for a good cause."

Clementine slid off her bar stool. "Lead the way."

The quaint Aurora mall was a short walk from the hotel. As they navigated the ice-slicked sidewalks—Anya a bit more masterfully than Clementine—they made a quick list of things necessary for a proper date. The outfit, of course. Possibly a handbag. And shoes. Who could forget shoes? By the time they entered the double doors of the mall's one large department store, Clementine realized she was in for a full-on girly shopping spree.

It was just what the doctor ordered.

Clementine was determined to enjoy herself. She refused to think about the plane ticket back to

Texas that was sitting on her dresser in the hotel room. Because now, when she boarded that plane, she wouldn't only be leaving the splendor of Alaska behind. She'd also be leaving Anya, Kodiak and Ben. And the rest of Aurora. The list was growing quite lengthy.

"What about this?" Anya held up a green dress with fluttery sleeves. "It would look great with your eyes."

"I don't know." Clementine ran her fingertips over the wispy fabric of the sleeves. "I might freeze to death."

"True. I forgot you're not acclimated quite yet."

Anya returned the dress to its rack and dived into a neighboring display. Clementine couldn't help but smile at the look of fierce determination on her face. Shopping for a date appeared to be serious business to Anya.

"Oh! Clementine, look at this." Her mouth spread into a satisfied grin as she spun around and presented another outfit.

This one was a fuzzy white sweater, sprinkled with crystals, and a long, matching wool skirt trimmed at the bottom with a thick band of faux fur. It was gorgeous.

Clementine bit her lip. "I love it. But will I look Alaskan or more like Mrs. Claus?"

"Neither." Anya thrust the ensemble toward her. "You'll look like a snow angel."

A snow angel. Clementine liked the sound of that.

Ben was taking her on a real date in this fantastic place—this winter wonderland known as Alaska. And she would look like a snow angel.

"So? What do you think?" Anya jiggled the hanger, and the crystals on the sweater glittered like diamonds.

A slow smile came to Clementine's lips. "It's perfect."

A proper date.

Dinner. Music. No dogs.

It sounded heavenly, at least to Clementine. She realized Nugget had a far different opinion, however, when she crawled under the bedspread and refused to come out.

Clementine checked on the stray husky to see if she, too, was staging a protest. The big dog remained stretched out, belly up, beneath the desk where Clementine sat when she worked on her research reports for the magazine.

"Thank you for being so understanding, Moose." Clementine gave the husky a pat on the head.

She hadn't wanted to name the dog, knowing it would only make turning her in to the shelter more difficult if Ben chose not to keep her. But it seemed so sad that she didn't have a name, not to mention impractical. And Moose suited the dog. Compared to Nugget, the stray was as big as one. Besides, it sounded Alaskan. So Clementine had christened her Moose.

"Nugget, it's only one night. I'll be home before you know it, and Moose is here to keep you company." Clementine stood beside the bed with her hands propped on her hips, and waited.

The lump under the bed covers shimmied closer to the foot of the bed. The Pomeranian was engaged in a world-class pout. Short of skipping her date entirely—which was *so* not an option—Clementine knew of only one way to remedy the situation.

"I'll bring you a doggy bag. How does that sound?"

The lump wiggled. Satisfied, Clementine grabbed her evening bag and slipped out the door. She knew the wag of a Pom tail when she saw one, even when it was hidden beneath a pile of blankets.

As she made her way downstairs, she couldn't help but wonder what Ben would look like dressed in something other than flannel. Her skirt swished around her legs with the heavy weight of the fur trim when she rounded the corner into the lobby. At first she didn't see Ben waiting for her beneath the outstretched paws of the polar bear. But when she passed the coffee bar, Anya flashed her a subtle thumbs-up and glanced toward the debonair man in the coat and tie—and Clementine did a double take.

Not only was he dressed in a slim-cut suit with a thin, black tie that emphasized his strapping shoulders, but he'd gone one step further in sprucing up for the evening.

He'd shaved. The beard was gone. In its place was a subtle dose of stubble, but by Alaskan standards, he was clean-shaven. As he watched her approach, he smiled, showing off his dimples and chiseled jaw, both now more visible than ever.

Clementine resisted the urge to run her fingertips over the smooth planes of his face when she reached his side. She clasped her beaded clutch to her chest in an attempt to hide the sudden hammering of her heart. "Hi, you."

Ben's gaze swept over her, and the appreciation in his blue eyes was obvious. He stared at her for what seemed like a full minute before he finally spoke. Even then, all he said was "Wow."

Pleasure warmed Clementine to her core, so she didn't hesitate when Ben asked if she would mind walking the few short blocks to the Aurora Convention Center for the banquet.

"Sure, let's walk."

"You won't be too cold?" Ben eyed her bare neck, exposed by her upswept hair, with concern.

Too cold? With the sparks of electricity bouncing between them? Doubtful. "I'll be fine."

"Good." His features relaxed into an easy, lopsided grin. "Because there's something I'd like to show you."

"That sounds oddly mysterious. Lead the way."

He helped her into her coat, gathered her hand in his and made sure she was tucked snugly by his side when they stepped into the night. Clementine gave Anya a wave goodbye as the revolving door spun closed behind them.

She barely wobbled on the icy pavement, even in her new shoes. Bunny boots might be practical, but they weren't exactly banquet material. She would have loved to wear a nice pair of glamorous stilettos. Real date shoes. Instead, she'd compromised and chosen a pair of creamy ivory suede boots with a wedge heel. Warm but feminine. Anya had even gone so far as to call them "subzero chic" when Clementine had modeled them in the department store.

"I hope you don't mind that I brought my camera. I might need to take a few photos for work while we're there." Ben bent his head toward her as he spoke. Warm clouds of his breath swirled between them.

Mmm. Minty. "Of course not. I'm glad you brought it. If you'd shown up minus the beard *and* the camera, I might wonder if it was really you."

He laughed and ran his free hand over his jaw. "You noticed the beard, huh?"

"Oh, yes. I noticed. What got into you? Isn't your face cold?"

She was only teasing him, so she was surprised when he turned serious eyes on her and answered, "It's been a while since I asked a woman on a date."

A while. She wondered what that meant. She felt sure there hadn't been a woman in his life since the accident.

Instead of asking these questions, she did what she'd decided to do every time she was tempted to worry about his past or his relationship with God. She prayed.

Lord, heal his heart.

A glimmer of hope burned in her chest. Ben had been up front with her. He admitted he had issues with God. He said he was angry and heartbroken about the loss of his dogs. He never implied he didn't believe in Him.

He was afraid. Clementine knew fear when she saw it. Ben was afraid to trust God. After what had happened to him out on the Bering Sea, she couldn't really blame him.

He gave her hand a gentle squeeze. "You've got to know I think you're special."

"I think you're pretty special yourself." Clementine felt as though she were walking on air as they passed the convention center and other happy, chattering couples stepping out of taxi cabs and onto the snowy sidewalk. "Where exactly are we going?"

He stopped and turned to face her. Even in her fancy wedged boots, the top of her head barely reached his nose. She tilted her face up toward his and tried not to let her gaze fall on his lips.

"Close your eyes," he murmured. "I'll lead you the rest of the way. We're almost there."

"Are you crazy?" She looked at the ground and the heaps of snow piled up on either side of the pavement. "I can't walk in this mess with my eyes closed. I can barely stand up straight with my eyes open."

He breathed out a sigh. "I'm not the only one

who's paranoid. Do I have to ask you again to trust me? I said shut your eyes."

She opened her mouth to protest again, but her words caught in her throat when he reached out and covered her eyes with his palm. His touch was tender, but his voice was firm. "Stop fighting me and close your eyes."

This time she did as he said, but not without releasing a frustrated lungful of air. She may have let Ben kiss her, but she still wasn't about to let him tell her what to do. "If I fall down in my new outfit, Ben Grayson…"

Her threat went unfinished and she let out a squeal as he wrapped his arms around her and swept her off her feet, quite literally. He carried her a dozen or so steps, then set her down as gently as if she were made of glass. He kept his arms wrapped around her and whispered in her ear, "Did you buy that beautiful dress to wear for me tonight?"

Warmth rose to Clementine's cheeks. She was aware of every frantic beat of her heart, echoing in her ears.

It's not a dress, she wanted to say. *It's a sweater and skirt.* But for once, she didn't feel like teasing him. "You shaved for me. I dressed for you. It's been a while for me, too."

"Looking at you here in the moonlight, and knowing you as I do, I find that awfully difficult to believe."

Her eyes still closed, her lips turned up in a bashful smile. It *had* been a while since she'd been on a date. Over a year since Mark. And it felt even longer. Not that she was complaining. She wanted to be alone.

She *had,* at least. Now she wasn't so sure.

She was a world away from anything she'd ever known. In Alaska, of all places. But she felt more alive than she ever had before. Everything else was beginning to take on a fuzzy quality in her mind, like an undeveloped photograph.

She thought about the Bible verse in 1 Corinthians 13: "Now we see but a poor reflection as in a mirror; then we shall see face to face." Looking at her past, everything that had happened—or, more accurately, *not* happened—before was like looking in a mirror. Now she was finally seeing God, and all He had for her, face to face.

Then she remembered the rest of that chapter and how it ended with "And now these three remain: faith, hope and love. But the greatest of these is love."

The greatest of these is love.

Clementine suddenly found it difficult to breathe. Love? She wasn't in love. She'd only known Ben a week. It couldn't be love.

"I'm opening my eyes now, whether you like it or not." She let her eyelashes flutter open and found Ben smiling at her. All the warmth in the world seemed to radiate from that smile.

The greatest of these is love.

He glanced over her shoulder. "Take a look around."

She almost didn't want to turn away. She would have been just fine to spend the rest of the evening looking at him, but she obediently spun around.

"Oh, Ben." Her hand flew to her chest.

He'd brought her to a small park, where a dozen or so ice sculptures stood, lit from below with colored spotlights. Glowing in the darkness were an enormous blue moose, a pink polar bear and a cool green eagle.

She walked at once to a violet sled dog running atop a frozen pedestal. Ethereal and graceful, it looked as though cut from amethyst gemstone. She reached toward the sculpture and gingerly placed her fingers on its back, and was almost surprised to find it icy cool to the touch.

"This is fantastic!"

At the exact moment Clementine peeked at Ben over her shoulder, he pressed the shutter button on his camera, capturing the moment.

"Sorry." He lowered the camera and winked. "You looked so enamored, I couldn't resist."

"I can't get over this place." She returned her gaze to the crystallized husky and decided it was very nearly life-sized. "How long will they last out here in the open?"

Ben shrugged. "As long as the temperature stays well below freezing, I think they'll be here awhile."

"Incredible." She shook her head. "And I can't believe we're the only ones out here."

He took a step closer. "I don't mind. Do you?"

"Not at all." She took her hand from the sculpture and let it fall on the smooth lapel of Ben's suit jacket.

His eyes, as clear and blue as ice, followed her every move as she reached up on her tiptoes, until her face was only inches from his.

"Thank you for bringing me here," she breathed. Then she leaned forward and rubbed her nose gently against his.

Ben's face split into a wide grin. "Did you just give me an Eskimo kiss?"

She bit her lip and shrugged. "When in Rome…"

"I've lived in Alaska my entire life and no one has ever given me an Eskimo kiss before."

"That seems a bit sad." She made tsk-tsk noises and gave him a look filled with mock sympathy.

He narrowed his gaze at her. "You know, that kind of kiss is actually called a *kunik* in Inuit. And it goes something more like this."

He cupped her cheeks with his hands and tipped her face toward his. Their eyes met and Clementine was instantly riveted. She had to remind herself to keep breathing as he pressed his nose and lips against her temple and slowly inhaled. His lips were surprisingly soft, and she could feel every warm puff of his breath dance across her skin.

They stayed that way for several moments, with the tip of his nose making a slow, tender trail up her temple toward her forehead. Their lips never touched, but it was the most meaningful kiss Clementine had ever experienced.

Once they'd found their seats in the maze of round banquet tables at the convention center, Ben pulled out Clementine's chair. She smiled at him over her shoulder and he could think of little else but their moment in the park.

She was exquisite, a treasure in his arms. After all the years he'd spent alone, he'd convinced himself he was better off that way. He didn't need a woman in his life.

Then along came Clementine and, with her charming way of putting him in his place, everything changed. He was growing accustomed to the idea of having her by his side. When she wasn't with him, he spent most of his time thinking about her, which posed a serious problem.

She was leaving in a matter of days. Ben raked a hand through his hair and sighed. He didn't even know exactly when she was scheduled to go home, but he knew the day was fast approaching.

He turned toward her and let his gaze fall on the side of her face. He was reminded instantly of her warm, vanilla scent and the way the soft curls falling from her upswept hair had tickled his nose. He cleared his throat and looked back down at his plate. "The race starts tomorrow."

"Yes, it does. I can't believe it's all happening so fast." She gestured toward the Gold Rush Trail start banner, draped across the stage at the front of the room. "Tomorrow I'll be standing underneath that banner on Main Street, handling a sled dog. I can't tell you how surreal that feels."

Despite the tug of worry that such an image conjured in his mind, he knew better than to voice his concerns. Besides, he'd seen her in action in the parking lot at her handling class and with Reggie's dogs when they'd gone mushing. She didn't look like a novice handler. Quite the opposite, in fact. "You'll do great. Just remember..."

"If I fall down, roll out of the way. I think I've got it." She laughed, then curled her hand around his. "Thanks for saying I'll do great. Your encouragement means a lot to me."

Ben squeezed her hand in return. And he found he couldn't hold back any longer—he had to ask. "When exactly do you need to go home?"

A look of confusion washed over her features, and she bit the corner of her lip. "Oh. You mean, home. As in Texas."

Texas. It sounded so far away. The word settled like a lead weight in the pit of his stomach. "Yes," he answered softly.

"I leave on Tuesday."

Three days.

When he'd checked into the Northern Lights Inn, he thought race week would last a lifetime. Now he wished he knew a way to slow the wheels of time and make it last even longer.

"Ma'am. Sir." A server stepped between them and placed their meals on the table.

Ben was thankful for the distraction. He had his answer. Clementine was scheduled to leave in three short days. He'd learned what he wanted to know.

And suddenly he had no appetite whatsoever.

He glanced over at Clementine, picking at the food on her plate with exploratory stabs of her fork. She looked even less interested in the food than he was. "Is everything okay?"

She dipped her head toward his. "I hate to be rude, but what exactly is this?" She gave her meat another poke and frowned at it.

Understanding suddenly dawned on him and he winced. "Caribou. They serve it at the banquet every year. It's a tradition."

Sure enough, she furrowed her brow. "I can't eat Rudolph, Ben."

"How do you know it's Rudolph? It could be Dancer. Or even Blitzen. One of the reindeer without top billing."

She lifted her fork, took a wary glance at it and brought it back down to her plate. "I don't think I can do it, even if it's Blitzen's distant cousin."

"Splitzen?"

She laughed. "So you've heard of him?"

"Sure. I know all about Splitzen." He gave her nose a playful tap. "Bobcats consider him a delicacy, you know."

Perhaps it was her laughter that gave him the

courage to bring up what would happen between them when she went home. Perhaps it was desperation. He couldn't be sure, but he took a deep breath and said it. "Clementine, I'd like us to keep in touch after you leave. I want you to know that."

Keep in touch? He cringed at his own words. He'd made it sound as though he wanted them to be pen pals. And that wasn't quite what he had in mind.

"Of course." Clementine looked down at her caribou. Was that a look of disappointment on her face?

Ben couldn't tell. He gave it another shot. "I hope we can see each other again."

"Me, too." Clementine's brow furrowed in apparent concentration. "I suppose there's always next year?"

Her words should have given him hope, but Ben felt anything but hopeful. Next year? He would have to wait twelve months to see her again?

A lot could happen in twelve months. People met and got married in twelve months. Would that happen with Clementine? And another man?

His mouth filled with a bitter taste and he glanced down at his plate. He shouldn't have said anything. What he'd wanted was for her to give him some kind of indication she wanted him to come visit. They'd joked about it before, but this was serious. She was about to leave the state. All she had to do was give him a hint that she wanted him to come and he'd be on the next plane with Kodiak.

Ben balled his hands into fists under the table.

What was he doing, making plans? Clementine hadn't said a word about his coming to see her in Texas.

Not that he blamed her. He couldn't make any promises about their future. Since the accident, it took every ounce of strength he could muster to get through one day at a time.

A change of subject was in order. Immediately, if not sooner. "Have you been assigned to a particular musher for tomorrow?"

"No. I'm just supposed to show up." She glanced at the stage, where one by one, the mushers were being introduced to the crowd. "I'm part of the pool of volunteer handlers who provide extra support. I'll be assigned to any musher who needs additional help."

"I hope you don't mind, but I spoke with a friend. Reggie Chase." Ben released her hand and reached into his suit pocket. "He said you could join his team as a handler if you like."

He pulled out an armband with the words *Musher Handler* emblazoned on it in red letters. Clementine's green eyes followed his every move as he unfolded it and pressed it into the palm of her hand.

Each musher in the Gold Rush Trail race was allowed to personally select a limited number of dog handlers for his team. Such spots had become coveted positions over the years. Musher handler armbands were typically only given to corporate sponsors, family members or close personal friends.

Ben wasn't sure if Clementine even knew the distinction between a musher handler and the other dog handlers, but he knew she would get more hands-on experience working with Reggie. And that sort of thing seemed important to her.

So it had become important to him as well. If thinking about it gave him an ulcer, so be it.

She pressed the armband to her heart and gazed at him with tear-filled eyes. "You did this? For me?"

The sight of her tears caused Ben's breath to catch in his throat. "Reggie's a great guy. You'll have a good time. Just promise me you'll be careful."

"I will."

A lone tear fell down her cheek, and Ben wiped it away with a brush of his thumb. "Would you like me to introduce you?"

"To Reggie? Now?" Clementine sat up straighter in her chair. The caribou and the matter of her leaving appeared to be forgotten.

Thank goodness.

"Yes." He nodded toward the cluster of tables near the front of the room where the mushers and their families were seated. "Don't you think it would be a good idea for the two of you to get acquainted before tomorrow?"

"Oh, yes."

He gestured toward her plate, where the caribou sat untouched. "Unless you'd like to finish your dinner first. I wouldn't want to come between you
     udolph."

She lifted an amused brow. "Rudolph's a little nonresponsive right now. I don't think he'll miss me."

"Okay, then," Ben said, grateful the awkward subject of their future had been dropped. "Let's go."

He helped her out of her chair and tried to let go of the nagging thought that nothing had changed. She was still leaving in three days, and he had no idea when he would see her again.

Chapter Eleven

Clementine followed Ben as he led her to a table directly in front of the stage. She did her best to concentrate on the people clustered around the table watching their approach, and not the way her hand felt in Ben's.

Cherished. As if it belonged there.

Stop it.

There was no use dwelling on such things. As they'd already established, she was leaving in three days. They wouldn't see one another for a year. Maybe never.

The thought gave her pause—along with a pang to her chest—so she pushed it away. It wasn't as if she could change things. She lived in Texas. Ben belonged in Alaska. End of story.

Stories could be rewritten, though, couldn't they?

"Clementine?"

She blinked, refocused and found Ben watching her with concern. She'd done it again—let her mind wander when she should have been paying attention to what was going on right in front of her. It was a good thing the bears in Alaska were hibernating. At the rate she was going, she would have walked right into one of them if they were out and about.

"Sorry." She gulped. "Distracted."

Ben gave her a knowing smile and wrapped his arm around her waist. She couldn't help but wonder if he was thinking about the same thing. Their relationship, for lack of a better term. Not the bears.

"Clementine, I'd like to introduce you to some friends of mine." He shifted his gaze to a man sitting at the table who had skin the color of warm caramel. "Reggie and Sue Chase."

Sue, who sat next to Reggie, had the same striking bone structure as Anya, except her complexion was darker, closer to her husband's. She wore a traditional Inuit hot-pink parka, with a large fur-trimmed hood. The parka was a pullover, more like a dress than a coat. Beside Sue, Clementine felt a bit ordinary, certainly not Alaskan.

Sue rose and wrapped her arms around her in a warm hug, as if she were an old friend. Clementine instantly felt at ease.

"We're so happy to meet you." Sue's dark eyes found Ben's for a moment and then flitted back to Clementine's. "Reggie and I have heard a lot about you."

"We sure have." Reggie stood beside his wife. He had a formidable black beard, like the musher on the Gold Rush Trail poster in the hotel lobby. A chunky silver-and-turquoise necklace in the shape of a sled dog team, complete with silver sled, wrapped around his thick neck. There was no mistaking this man was a dog musher.

He, too, gave Clementine a fierce hug.

"I'm pleased to meet you both." Her voice was muffled against his shoulder until he released her.

"Sit down." Sue waved to their empty chairs. "Join us."

"We can't take your seats, Sue." Ben pulled Clementine next to him again, as though she belonged with him.

Sue and Reggie must have noticed because they shared a knowing glance and a smile.

"Sure you can." Reggie grabbed Ben by the shoulders and pushed him into one of the chairs. "Sit. I'll go dig up a few more chairs. I'm still a musher, you know. I have some clout around here."

It was only a vague reference to Ben's past, but it made Clementine's breath catch in her throat. She sank into the chair beside Ben's and glanced at him. She breathed easier when she saw how relaxed he looked. Obviously he and Reggie were close. The fact that Reggie wasn't afraid to mention Ben's experience as a musher told her as much. She doubted Ben would tolerate it from anyone else.

"Reggie was there for me," Ben said in a low tone, so only Clementine could hear. "After the accident, I mean."

She nodded, glad that Ben hadn't had to go through such a tragedy alone. In the hours since he'd told her about losing his dog team, Clementine had thought a lot about his cabin in the woods, specifically the graveyard of empty doghouses. She couldn't understand how he could live there every day. She realized now, after meeting Reggie and Sue, that his isolation was a choice. Ben wanted to cut himself off from people. That's why he stayed out there.

Is that why he kissed me? Because I'm leaving soon? I won't stay around to complicate things. He can go back to his lonely life as soon as I'm gone.

She didn't want to believe it. He'd already told her he wanted to see her again, after she'd left Alaska. He'd told her she was special. And here he was introducing her to his friends.

An image of Mark riding around on that ridiculous motorcycle flashed in her mind. As much as she hated to admit it, things weren't always as they seemed. And sometimes people weren't who they seemed, either. The mess with Mark had taught her that much.

Sue pulled a chair next to hers while Reggie sat on Ben's other side. "Clementine, I hear you're going to help Reggie tomorrow with his dog team."

"Yes." Clementine thought about the musher handler armband tucked away in her handbag and at once felt reassured. Ben cared about her, even if she was leaving soon. "I'm really looking forward to it. Are you going to be helping out with Reggie's dogs as well?"

"No. I belong to a group of mushers' wives who provide hospitality at the race start."

"Hospitality?"

"We pass out hot chocolate and apple cider so spectators can stay warm." Sue nodded toward the slide show flashing images of one frigid scene after another on a big screen suspended above the stage.

Clementine shuddered. "You keep everyone warm. That seems like an awfully tall order."

Sue laughed. "I guess you could say we're only moderately successful."

"I think it's great how the whole community comes together to support the race."

"The race couldn't go on without all the volunteers. And the mushers certainly couldn't brave the Alaskan wilderness alone. Everyday life in Aurora stops for the duration of the race. We all pitch in and do whatever is necessary to keep everyone safe—dogs and people alike." Sue swelled with pride for her town when she spoke.

And Clementine couldn't help but feel the tiniest bit envious. Houston was a big city. On any given day, people moved about without any thought to what their neighbors were doing. She wondered what it would be like to live somewhere like Aurora.

Nice. It would most definitely be nice.

The thought made her all warm inside, like she'd just had one of Anya's flavored coffees.

Ben rose from the table and nudged his way between Clementine and Sue. "What are you two talking about over here? You're not giving away all my secrets, are you?"

He looked at Sue with mock consternation and then winked at Clementine.

Her insides instantly grew even warmer. "She's told me everything. I've got all sorts of blackmail now."

"I should have known better than to leave the two of you alone."

"We were good. I promise." Sue held up her right hand. "Scout's honor."

Ben narrowed his gaze at her. "When were you a scout?"

She shrugged. "Never."

"That's what I thought." He chuckled as he took Clementine's hand and lifted her out of her seat. "We're going to take a look around the auction. That is, unless you two need more time to slander me."

Sue rolled her eyes.

Clementine laughed as he escorted her to the auction tables to the right side of the stage. As much as she enjoyed talking to Sue, she was glad to be back at Ben's side. "Just so you know, we weren't talking about you. Sue was telling me all about Aurora."

He gave her a questioning glance as he tucked her arm through his. "And what did you think?"

"I love it here." She sighed. "Then again, I already knew that."

* * *

She loves it here. She loves Alaska.

Against his better judgment, Ben found himself wondering if she would ever stay. He couldn't come out and ask her, but the question burned in his gut.

He did his best to ignore it and instead focused on the silent auction items and sales table. An assortment of autographed race bibs, commemorative posters from prior years and dog booties lined the tables up and down the ballroom. After Ben told Clementine people sometimes used the dog booties as cell phone or iPod covers, she purchased five to bring home as gifts. The older gentleman behind the cash register grinned and asked her if she had a five-legged dog, which prompted her to laugh and toss her hair in a way that alleviated any lingering worries Ben had been holding on to.

"Wait a sec." She paused before moving on to the higher-end auction items and unzipped her tiny purse. It was far too small to hold a dog, so there was no way Ben could be mistaken about the fact that it was a purse and not a dog carrier. "I want to put my cell phone in one of these."

She slipped her phone in a black dog booty with a lime-green band and Velcroed it closed.

When it didn't quite fit back in her minuscule bag, Ben said, "Here, let me."

He slid the phone, booty and all, into his coat pocket.

"Thanks." She slipped her arm through his as

they continued to browse. "You know, you're quite the gentleman."

Ben said nothing, but he lifted her hand and gave it a tender kiss.

Clementine's cheeks took on a rosy hue. She gave him a bashful smile before taking a glance at the display tables. "Oh, my. Look at that."

He followed her gaze to a sapphire-blue parka with an enormous silver fur ruff.

She lifted the sleeve and held it against her cheek. "It's velvet."

The woman manning the auction table smiled at Ben and removed the parka from its display hanger. "It's completely handmade. All Native craftsmanship." She held it toward Clementine. "Would you like to try it on?"

Clementine glanced at the clipboard with the long list of handwritten bids for the parka. "Oh, no. I couldn't."

"Go ahead." Ben nodded toward the coat. "What's the harm in trying it on?"

She looked longingly at it. "Well, okay."

She slipped her arms into the sleeves and wrapped the plush velvet around her slender form. The parka was a perfect fit. Not only that, it was stunning on her. She looked like some kind of snow queen. Ben found it suddenly difficult to swallow.

The auction woman beamed. "You look beautiful."

An understatement if Ben had ever heard one.

He reached for his camera. Clementine peeked at him over the silver fur. He couldn't even see her nose or lips. Only her eyes…those luminous eyes.

He snapped her picture.

"It's made for you, dear." The woman at the table nodded and held her hand to her heart. "And it's so warm. It would be perfect for Nome."

At the mention of Nome, Ben's heart plummeted. He looked at Clementine over the top of his camera and their eyes met. And in that moment, he knew.

She wanted to stay.

Wordlessly, she removed the coat. Ben busied himself with putting away his camera. He didn't trust himself to even look in her direction. Nor did he check the photo he'd taken of her on the camera's digital display. He couldn't take it.

He heard a buzzing noise, dragging him from his thoughts of Nome, and realized it was coming from his suit pocket.

"I think your phone is ringing." He fished her cell phone, complete with dog booty, from his pocket and handed it to her.

"It's the hotel." She frowned as she looked at the small, illuminated screen on the vibrating phone. "Hello?"

Ben watched her face crumple.

"Oh, no. And no one has seen her?" She reached for her throat, with an unmistakable tremor in her hands. "We'll be right there."

Tears pooled in her eyes as she ended the call.

Ben slipped his arm around her shoulders. "What is it?"

"It's Nugget." She clutched the cell phone and blinked up at him. "She's missing."

Chapter Twelve

"I don't understand how this could have happened. They said she darted out the door when house-keeping went into my room for turndown service. I thought I put the do-not-disturb sign on the door." Clementine rushed out of the convention center, toward the Northern Lights Inn. From a few blocks away, it looked so cozy. A ribbon of smoke curled from its chimney and the windows, rimmed with snow, glowed with a friendly, gold warmth.

The quaint scene did little to quell her worry. Somewhere inside that building, her tiny dog was lost.

"We'll find her." Ben gave her hand a reassuring squeeze and she glanced over at him.

He looked so strong, so certain.

Her frantic heartbeat slowly returned to normal.

"She was upset that I left her behind." Clementine shook her head. "I promised her a doggy bag. I totally forgot."

"I promised Kodiak the same thing. I've got the leftover caribou all wrapped up in my camera bag." Ben ran his thumb in soothing circles over the back of her hand. "He can share."

"Thank you."

She tried to tell herself that everything was going to be fine. They would get back to the hotel and it would all be some sort of mix-up. Nugget would be in her room, right where Clementine had left her. Moose would be there, too, watching over Nugget like a big, furry protector. Maybe she and Ben could bring the dogs down to the lobby and feed them the leftovers while they shared a coffee and snuggled on the big, comfy sofa.

Please, God. Please let it be so.

She blinked back a fresh wave of tears and quickened her pace, although it was easier said than done on the icy pavement. She reached for the reassurance of the cross on the chain around her neck and nearly stumbled.

Ben caught her and eyed her with concern. "Try not to worry. Everything is going to be fine."

Everything is going to be fine. Exactly the words she so desperately needed to hear.

She clung to them.

Ben watched Clementine reach for her necklace while he wrapped his arm around her waist. As her fingertips clutched the dainty gold cross, it came to him.

He knew exactly what would make Clementine feel better about Nugget. Perhaps they could pray together for Nugget's safe return.

He shifted from one foot to the other and fought the impulse to ignore the idea and keep walking to the hotel.

Everything within him railed against it. Could he really pour his heart out to God in front of Clementine? Even if he could, would God really listen?

Part of him thought their time would be better spent getting back to the hotel to search for Nugget. His prayers would be of no use. He hadn't uttered a proper prayer in years. He wouldn't know what to say, where to begin. Just because he'd been reading his Bible lately didn't mean he expected God to be there when he needed Him, did it?

No. I just...can't.

He gathered Clementine next to him and took a step in the direction of the Northern Lights Inn. But his feet refused to move an inch. Clementine peered up at him, her eyes wide with worry. Her full bottom lip trembled, and Ben knew giving up on the idea was a lost cause.

He would do it simply because it would alleviate her worry. And maybe, just maybe, God would hear him.

"Clementine, would you like to pray? For Nugget, I mean?" he finally asked, in a voice gruff with emotion.

Visible relief coursed through her, and she smiled at him in spite of her tears. "Yes, I would. Thank you."

Her lip wobbled again, and shame pierced Ben's soul. How could he have almost pushed down the instinct to pray? He could do this. *Would* do this. For her.

He was the first to close his eyes, the first to speak. He had no clue how to start, but he figured saying anything, simply asking for help, would make her feel better.

"Lo-ord." His voice cracked.

Get a grip on yourself.

He cleared his throat and continued. "Clementine's little dog is missing. Nugget. I'm asking You to help us find her. Please keep her safe. And keep Clementine from worrying too much."

He opened his eyes a fraction and took her in, with her bowed head and soft curls framing her face.

Then he closed his eyes again and finished with, "She loves You. Amen."

He waited to see if she would add anything of her own. She clasped his hands a bit tighter, and he realized one of them was trembling. He wasn't even sure if it was him or her.

Then she spoke with remarkable calm. Her voice was softer than a lullaby. "Father, Your Word says that if two of us on Earth agree about anything we ask for, if will be done. For where two or three come

together in Your name, You are there with them. You
are here right now, with Ben and me."

She paused and the air between them grew still,
silent.

Ben couldn't hear a thing—not even the arctic
wind that whipped his coattails—other than his own
heart. It beat loud and strong, filling his ears. It beat
so hard that it ached. He told himself it couldn't
be true. God wasn't here on a lonely sidewalk in
Aurora. But the pounding of his rebellious heart
told him he wanted to believe it.

"So we ask that You lead us to Nugget and protect her wherever she is. In Christ's name we pray.
Amen."

Clementine's eyes opened. Ben, suddenly acutely
self-conscious, switched his gaze to his feet. "I hope
that was…"

His voice trailed off. He'd never felt more out of
his element.

"It was perfect. Thank you." She dragged his attention away from his shoes with a gentle kiss on
the cheek.

He looked up, met her gaze once more and took
in her bittersweet smile. And, just like that, any lingering awkwardness between them melted away.

He motioned toward the hotel, a mere block or so
away. "Shall we?"

She nodded and they headed toward the Northern Lights Inn, hand in hand. It wasn't a leisurely
stroll, but Clementine's steps were slower, less fran-

tic than they had been before. Ben couldn't deny that the prayer had brought a certain sense of peace to the situation.

But with it came a gnawing doubt in Ben's gut.

He was convinced they would find the dog. He wouldn't stop looking until she was safe and sound in Clementine's arms. He knew he couldn't bear the heartrending look in her eyes so long as Nugget was missing. Now, he also had the added element of the prayer to worry about. Clementine didn't deserve to lose her dog, and she most certainly didn't deserve to lose her faith. Or even a tiny part of it.

Jaw clenched, Ben waged a silent war with God in his thoughts.

Lord, don't let her down. Bring the dog back.

Begging was out of the question. He refused to resort to such desperate measures. But the minute they pushed through the revolving doors of the hotel his resistance wavered.

Please.

"Ben, look!" Clementine dropped his hand and ran toward the registration desk.

He followed, ducking when her path brought his head perilously close to the polar bear's threatening claws. She stopped short when she reached the desk, and Ben skidded to a halt behind her.

Likewise, his heart slammed into his rib cage when he spotted a familiar ball of fluff over Clementine's shoulder.

"Nugget?" He frowned at the Pomeranian, resting on a blanket spread across the check-in counter. The little dog wagged her tail and let out a yip.

Of course it was Nugget. Who else would it be? It's not like the state of Alaska was crawling with lapdogs.

Clementine scooped the dog into her arms and grinned at him like crazy over the top of Nugget's fuzzy head. "She's here."

"She certainly is." The hotel manager came around the front of the desk, holding a folded newspaper. "I'm Bob Easton. You must be Clementine. And you are?"

"Ben Grayson." Ben shook the man's hand but scarcely took in his presence. He couldn't take his eyes off Clementine and her dog. "Was she ever really lost?"

"Most definitely. A member of our housekeeping staff found her only a few minutes ago, cowering in a supply closet."

A few minutes ago. While they'd been praying.

It didn't mean anything. Coincidences like this happened all the time.

Still, Ben had difficulty concentrating on the conversation. They hadn't even had to look for the dog. They'd just walked in and she was sitting right there. Waiting.

"A supply closet?" Clementine winced. "I'm so sorry. And my other dog? Moose?"

The hotel manager gave her a reassuring nod.

"Safe and sound in your room. She never so much as budged."

Moose?

So now the stray had a name.

Ben figured he may as well cave and tell Clementine he would take the dog. It felt like Moose already had one paw firmly wedged in his life. Resistance was futile where Clementine was concerned.

"Thank you for looking after her up here." Clementine smiled at Bob Easton as she snuggled Nugget close to her chest. "I told the person who called me earlier to just put her back in my room if she was found."

"Oh, I couldn't do that. Nugget here is a celebrity." Bob scratched Nugget under her minuscule chin.

Clementine flushed and lowered her voice. "Celebrity? Oh, no. Did everyone in the building hear about her getaway?"

Bob let out a hearty laugh and gave Ben a knowing look, as if he were in on some kind of joke. "Not that. I'm talking about this."

He unfolded the newspaper and held it toward Clementine. The *Yukon Reporter*. Early edition. With one of Ben's own photographs on the front page.

"What is this?" Clementine furrowed her brow and looked back and forth between Ben and the image of Nugget, nearly life-sized, directly beneath the masthead. She was half-buried in snow, but her pink bunny slippers were clearly visible. "Is this from the other day, before the snowball fight?"

Ben took the paper from Bob, who was being paged to help out with another crisis. Something about a leaking toilet. "Yes. I hope you don't mind. I was going to tell you before it came out, but I thought it might be a fun surprise."

Nugget stared at the newspaper, as if looking into a mirror. Clementine read the photo caption aloud. "*Nugget, a Pomeranian from Texas, enjoys the snow just days before the Gold Rush Trail sled dog race.*"

A slow smile came to her lips. "My dog is fine. And she's on the front page of the paper."

Ben didn't even want to address Nugget's disappearing act. He was still trying to make sense of the entire episode. "Don't be too impressed. It's a small-town paper, remember. Our circulation isn't very big."

"That doesn't matter, silly." She swatted him with the newspaper and Nugget flinched in her arms. "I look at pictures for a living. Pictures of other people, doing exciting things in other places. Never anything to do with me. And now, look. My dog. On the front page. This is crazy. I don't even know what to say."

She shook her head and stared, transfixed, at the photo.

Ben could hardly believe it. He'd rendered her speechless, a feat he'd considered impossible until now. When Clementine spoke her mind she was a force to be reckoned with. A silent Clementine was like the dawn after a storm. Serene, thoughtful. But no less fascinating.

He cupped her chin and captured her gaze. "So you like it, then?"

"I do," she answered.

Just like a bride.

Chapter Thirteen

Everything about race day was more intense than Clementine could have imagined. The dogs were louder. The crowds were bigger. The weather was colder.

The lights along Main Street, all decorated with Gold Rush Trail banners, cast a dim glow over the snow-covered street. Everything—the snow, the sky, the white awnings covering the hot chocolate stands where Sue and other musher wives handed out cocoa and cider—had taken on an almost-eerie violet hue in the predawn hours.

Clementine's fingers nearly froze when she removed her gloves long enough to strap on her musher handler armband. With the armband firmly in place, and a fresh swarm of butterflies taking flight in her belly, she marched over to the dog handler headquarters with Anya.

"Headquarters" consisted of a red pickup truck with chains on the tires and a bright orange flag that would have whipped around in the bitter wind if not for the fact that it was frozen stiff. On the passenger-side window, someone had taped the musher roster that had been printed in the early edition of the paper. There was a photo of each musher, along with the team's race number.

Clementine had already read all about Reggie in the newspaper with Nugget's photo. After she and Ben had watched Nugget, Kodiak and Moose devour the contents of the doggy bag—clearly those three didn't have any qualms about eating Rudolph's relatives—they'd ordered coffee, settled on the sofa beneath the giant moose head and talked late into the evening. Reggie and Sue had stopped by for a bit and Anya had joined them after her shift ended, but Clementine and Ben had closed the place down. She'd gone back to her room exhausted but full of breathless excitement. She'd spread the newspaper on her bed and pored over Reggie's bio. Anything to make the night last longer. She was afraid to go to bed, lest she wake in the morning to find it was all a dream.

The chattering of her teeth told her it was most definitely not a dream. She was really in Aurora, Alaska. The days were passing with alarming speed, but they had yet to run out.

"Hey, Anya. Good morning, Clementine." Aidan stood in the bed of the truck, armed with a wide smile and a bullhorn. "Today's the big day. Are you two ready?"

He looked even younger than he had at dog handling class. Maybe it was the bullhorn. He wielded it like a kid with a shiny new toy.

"Sure am," Anya replied with a confidence that Clementine couldn't help but envy.

"I'm ready." Clementine gave the thumbs-up sign. Now that her hands were warm and safe in her gloves again, the feeling had returned to her fingers. "Stop, drop and roll."

Aidan just shook his head. "Whatever. Try not to get hurt."

"Yes, sir." The act of calling him "sir" was enough to make her giggle.

"So I see you've found your way onto a musher's team." He motioned toward her armband.

"Yes. Reggie Chase." Clementine nodded toward the roster, where she easily spotted Reggie's dark skin and thick beard among the collection of small headshots. The square grid of photos looked like a sheet of mountain man postage stamps. "Number fifty-eight."

"Cool." Aidan squatted and held out a clipboard for her inspection. "This is the map of the area. Reggie's team should be getting ready over on Third. Anya, why don't you hang out here until one of the mushers calls for help."

"Will do." She nodded. "Have fun, Clementine."

The starting line for the race was at the corner of Main and First. The first ten teams lined up on Main, in numerical order for about six city blocks.

The remaining teams waited on the surrounding side streets until given the signal to pull out onto Main. Clementine studied the map and headed off to Third Street after promising Anya she would have a good time and again reassuring Aidan she would stop, drop and roll if things got out of control.

The sun was coming up, changing the sky from wild violet to soft pink. Clementine was grateful for the warmth of the sun's rays filtering through the light snowfall. Okay, so maybe it wasn't warmth per se, but her nose was a little less numb. That had to be a good sign.

The bib numbers were written in large black letters on paper plates, which had been stapled to posts and plunged into the snow banks. Musher trucks lined the streets, parked beside the paper plate markers, with the dogs tethered to the vehicles. Some of the dogs seemed to take all the chaos in stride and rested on beds of straw, with their eyelids fighting to stay open. Other dogs bounced at the end of their leashes, anxious to make the trip through the Aurora streets and head into the wilderness of the trail.

Clementine took it all in, trying to memorize every detail. She watched as camera crews swarmed around musher number 13, Mackey Brewer, the previous year's champion. She squinted, trying to find Ben among the throng of photographers. She gasped when instead she spotted a television cameraman wearing a baseball cap emblazoned with the familiar *Nature World* logo.

Her first instinct was to look away. Pretend she hadn't seen it. As if spotting something so closely associated with her real life would whisk her away, like a click of Dorothy's ruby-red slippers.

This is ridiculous.

Like a magnet, her gaze was drawn back to the logo. She let her eyes wander to the photographer's face. He looked right back at her. Correction: through her. Of course he didn't recognize her. Why would he? He was a nature photographer and she was a nameless, faceless cubicle dweller. It wasn't as if they would have crossed paths anywhere.

All those years behind that desk. And for what?

She pushed the question away, determined not to ruin the start of the race with negative thoughts. She marched over, introduced herself to the photographer and showed him her *Nature World* press credentials. He took down the information she provided about Reggie Chase and promised to get some shots of her assisting with his dogs.

Clementine hoped he would, in fact, return. He seemed much more interested in joining the horde of reporters and photographers surrounding Mackey Brewer. She watched, worried as he disappeared into the crowd.

"Clementine?" Reggie, clad in a traditional Native anorak and enormous mittens made of some sort of animal hide, appeared from behind a nearby truck and appraised her with his black eyes.

Clementine glanced at the paper plate noting his

parking space. Sure enough, number 58. He was right where Aidan had said she could find him. "Hi, Reggie."

She offered her hand, but he ignored it and instead enveloped her in a tight hug.

He had no problems speaking through the thick fur ruff of his anorak. "Welcome to the team."

"Thanks again for having me." A few of the butterflies in her stomach fluttered away. Reggie, once again, was all smiles and warm welcome.

He held her at arm's length and patted her shoulders with his massive mittens. "Sue says you're the one."

Clementine looked around at the other handlers milling around, wondering if he'd gotten her confused with someone else. A super-handler of some sort. "Um, I'm not quite sure what you mean."

"You're the one." He winked. His dark lashes were coated with a fine dusting of snow powder.

"The one?" she repeated. Saying it aloud didn't make his meaning any clearer.

"The one who's bringing my boy Ben back to life." He whacked her on the back and a hearty laugh bubbled up his throat.

The one. As in The One?

A warm glow came over Clementine. She dipped her chin, embarrassed by the flush that she knew had made its way to her cheeks. Surely that's not what he meant. "Bringing him back to life?"

"Yes. I wondered what it would take to get him

back on track." Reggie shook his head. "I never thought it would be a woman. Never thought he would find someone, seeing as he's practically turned into a hermit. The Lord does indeed work in mysterious ways."

Clementine wondered just what Sue, or possibly Ben himself, had told Reggie. Whatever it was, it warmed her heart to hear his friend quote Scripture. Perhaps he'd prayed for Ben, just as she had. "You're a believer?"

"Yes, ma'am." He looked off into the distance where the streets of Aurora disappeared into the horizon and a line of snow-laden evergreens sat at the base of the Chugach Mountains. "It would be foolish to get on a sled and ride it into the unknown if I didn't trust in Him to pull me through."

Clementine wasn't sure why, but she felt compelled to tell Reggie what she knew about Ben's past. "Ben told me about his accident."

Reggie didn't seem at all surprised at this revelation. "Our boy Ben thinks God let him down. One day he'll come to understand what really happened four years ago. Ben lost most of his team, but his life was spared. God saved him."

His words touched a tender place inside Clementine. "He feels responsible."

"Any musher would. The bond between a musher and his dogs is a strong one." Reggie was a musher through and through. So was Ben. Of that, Clementine was certain.

She could only pray that Ben would one day trust in God enough to return to that life. Experiencing it with him had given her a tiny taste of what such a life must have been like for him. She had seen the way the tension had disappeared from his handsome features when he stood on the sled runners. She knew he missed it.

The loss of Ben's team was second only to the loss of years the tragedy had brought. Four years had passed. How much longer would he wait?

Reggie took a sidelong glance at Clementine. When he spoke, it was as if he could read her thoughts. "Ben will come back to it someday. 'I will repay you for the years the locusts have eaten.' Joel 2:25. One of my favorite promises in all of God's Word."

"I will repay you for the years the locusts have eaten," Clementine repeated. The verse brought a trail of goose bumps up and down her arms.

"God will restore Ben's lost years. Have faith." Reggie pointed one of his furry mittens toward the sky. "It will happen."

I will repay you for the years the locusts have eaten. It was a lovely promise, one that Clementine would hold on to. A feeling of overwhelming gratitude came over her. There were other people praying for Ben.

As comforting as she found this, Clementine didn't feel right talking about Ben behind his back. "What can I do to help you, Reggie?"

He pulled off a mitten and removed a tube filled with some sort of bright pink gel from his pocket. He tossed it to Clementine. "Here. Rub some of this paw ointment on the dogs' pads for me, would you? I'll get started harnessing them up."

The irony of his request didn't escape her. Paw ointment. She wished Ben were here. He'd probably be laughing, his freshly shaved face creased with dimples and his eyes crinkled in the corners.

She opened the tube and went to work applying the ointment to each of the dogs' paws. Another handler followed, fastening booties into place.

"Dogs lose booties all the time," Reggie explained. "Exposed paws will crack and bleed if not protected. That's where the ointment comes in."

"I see." Clementine felt a little guilty for teasing Ben about the whole ointment thing. He was right. It was an important part of the race.

As if on cue, she heard the whir of a camera shutter and his familiar rugged voice behind her. "What do we have here?"

She turned, careful not to lose the grip she had on one of the lead dog's back feet.

Sure enough, there stood Ben, grinning from ear to ear. "Is that my Clementine with paw ointment on her hands?"

My Clementine. Her heart skipped a beat. *The One.*

She straightened and aimed an accusatory glare at him. "You put him up to this, didn't you?"

"I have no idea what you're talking about." His features fell into a look of mock innocence, but a mischievous glint danced in his eyes.

"Ben Grayson, I cannot believe you."

He snapped another picture. "Has anyone ever told you how stunning you look when you're angry?"

She wasn't angry. She was delighted. She hadn't expected to see him before the start of the race. "I'm bundled up from head to toe and my hands are covered in a greasy mess. I'm hardly stunning."

"I have proof." He tapped the lens of his camera. "You're breathtaking."

"You don't look half bad yourself. The clean-shaven look suits you."

"My face is frozen." He ran a gloved hand over his chin. "I can't feel a thing, but thanks."

"Hey, there, Ben." Reggie walked past them, stretching out the gang line and laying it on the ground. It painted a bright blue streak in the snow. "Thanks for sending me Clementine. She's a natural. Got everyone set with ointment in no time flat."

"Paw ointment is kind of my specialty." She winked at Ben. Or at least she gave it an attempt. Her face was so numb from the cold that she couldn't be sure if it actually moved.

She realized the effort must have been a success when he winked back.

"You ready to babysit a pair of dogs until it's time to go?" Reggie nodded toward the huskies, now straining at their leads to get to the gang line.

"I sure am." Clementine took a deep breath. The frigid air burned her lungs but she hardly noticed. She'd come so far. And here she was—about to help lead a dog team to the start of the Gold Rush Trail.

"Come on over here." He lifted the pair of neck lines closest to the sled. "The pair of dogs that go here are called the wheel dogs. You're my wheel dog handler. Got it?"

"Got it." She held on the tug line while Reggie connected one of the wheel dogs to its neck line.

Ben wordlessly went to work attaching the other dog in place. Clementine watched his fingers move over the equipment with expert speed and precision. His gaze swept over each fastener, one at a time, checking and double-checking the cables. She wondered if he had any idea how at ease he looked. Much more so than he looked with a camera strapped around his neck.

Reggie returned and set serious eyes on Ben. "Thanks for the help, friend." He motioned toward the pair of dogs standing between them. "These are two great athletes, but Kodiak was always the best wheel dog a musher could have."

The three of them stood there for what seemed like an eternity, none of them uttering a word, while the wheel dogs worked themselves up into a frenzy.

At last Ben simply turned on his heel and walked away.

Clementine followed him with her gaze, tracing his slumped shoulders and downcast eyes.

"Don't mind him. He'll get over it." Reggie waved a dismissive hand toward the street corner where Ben turned and disappeared without a backward glance. "He doesn't like to talk about the past."

She bit her lip and blinked back the tears collecting behind her eyes. Tears for Ben.

She didn't have the luxury of time to get her emotions under control. Reggie was already poised on the sled runners, ready to give the Hike command and swish through the snow toward the start line. Clementine's stomach churned and she couldn't help but marvel at Reggie's calm confidence. Her job would be over in a matter of minutes, but his was only beginning. For the next ten days, he would know only the sled, his dogs and the tough Alaskan wilderness. She couldn't imagine facing such uncertainty.

And to think Ben had ever done such a thing caused a shiver to run up her spine. A shiver that had nothing to do with the cold.

"Reggie?" she called out to him, above the barking madness of sixteen anxious sled dogs.

He smiled at her, and the fiery spark in his dark eyes told her he was just as eager as his dog team to get out on the trail. "Yes?"

"I'll be praying for you to get to Nome safely."

"Thanks. God willing, I'll see you there." He pointed toward her musher handler armband, strapped around the left sleeve of her parka. "Keep that. You can help care for my dogs in Nome."

"Oh, I'm not going to Nome." A week ago, Nome didn't mean a thing to her. All she cared about was the start of the race. Now she could think of nowhere else she'd rather be two days from now.

However was she going to go back to her cubicle? What would she be doing when Reggie crossed the finish line? Sorting through piles of photographs of places she would never go? Eating another Lean Cuisine?

Missing Ben, she thought. *I'll be missing Ben. And Alaska.*

Reggie shrugged and said with a grin, "Plans change. Keep the armband."

Plans change.

She opened her mouth, fully prepared to tell him things were never that simple, but before she could say a word it was time.

"Hike."

Reggie didn't need to repeat the command. Clementine barely had time to tighten her grip on the gang line before she felt herself being pulled through the snow. The sheer power of the dogs lifted her clear off her feet, and she realized all those practice loops around the Northern Lights Inn parking lot bore little resemblance to the real deal.

Her heart beat faster and faster, in perfect rhythm with the swift steps of the wheel dogs. Clementine ran with all her might, determined to keep up with the team. By the time they reached the starting line, she wasn't sure if she'd run the three blocks down

Main Street or simply been part of an unstoppable freight train of momentum.

As soon as the lead dog crossed the shadow of the start banner, slung overhead between two lamp-posts, Reggie called out, "Whoa!"

Clementine considered it nothing less than a miracle when the sixteen dogs all slowed to a stop. She bent over, gasping for breath and choked when the stinging arctic air hit her lungs. Reggie's name and bib number were announced over a loud speaker, and a roar went up from the crowd. The wheel dogs swiveled their heads in unison and looked at Clementine as if asking permission to run again.

Clementine ran her hand under their chins and cooed, "Just a minute longer guys. Be patient."

They whined and pawed at the frosty ground as the countdown began.

10...9...8...

Clementine looked around at the swarms of people lined up on either side of the chute, cheering and chanting Reggie's name. She tried to find Ben in the throng of photographers jockeying for position up and down the orange plastic fencing. She thought she spied him up near Reggie's lead dog, lying on his stomach in the snow, aiming his camera straight at the dogs. She couldn't be sure. The camera, with its bulky telephoto lens, covered most of his face.

Of course it's him. She swallowed the lump in her throat. *He's hiding behind that lens.*

7...6...5...

An eerie quiet fell over the team, and she had no problem hearing Reggie when he said her name in his calm, still voice. "Clementine."

"Yes?"

4…3…2…

"In his heart a man plans his course, but the Lord determines his steps."

1.

And he was gone, nothing more than a flurry of snow whooshing past her in a blur.

Chapter Fourteen

The morning after the race began, a quietness came over the Northern Lights Inn. Ben should have grown accustomed to it by now, but it always took him by surprise. During the years he'd spent as the one on the sled runners mushing a team toward Nome, he'd come to know this time as one of intense concentration, fueled by a heavy dose of adrenaline. The hush at race headquarters stood in such stark contrast that he'd never quite come to expect it.

The lobby was a ghost town. He sat by the large stone fireplace warming his hands, with Kodiak curled at his feet. He'd been up late sorting through hundreds upon hundreds of photographs. It had been close to midnight when he'd made his final selection of which pictures to send to his editor. The quiet morning would have been the perfect time to sleep in and get caught up on his rest. But resting didn't come easy. What little sleep he did manage to get was plagued with dreams of the trail. And in the hours he spent awake, his thoughts always came back to Clementine.

The way she'd watched him when he helped get Reggie's dogs attached to the gang line haunted him. She hadn't said a word, but he'd seen the thoughts behind her beautiful green eyes.

She thought he should be the one riding that sled into Nome.

She'd never pushed. Her restraint stood in stark contrast to her customary teasing way of dealing with things. Her tender silence on the matter gave her opinion all the more force. It had hit Ben like a punch straight to the gut. All she'd done was asked him if he missed it when he finally broke down and told her about the accident. And he'd told her the truth. No, he hadn't missed it.

Until she came along.

What kind of woman could inspire a man to do the one thing that terrified him most?

A woman like Clementine, Ben admitted with a sigh.

Kodiak rested his chin on Ben's knee and fixed his gold eyes on his master's face, as if he knew what Ben was contemplating.

Now that Ben thought about it, the dog probably did know. Kodiak knew him better than anyone, human or canine. He had been by Ben's side through it all. He was the living, breathing embodiment of the phrase "man's best friend."

Ben knew this might seem unusual, or even sad,

to some people but it was enough for him. Rather, it had been until a certain God-fearing, adventure-loving tourist with an affection for bunny slippers came along.

"What do you think, boy?" Ben ran his thumb along the ridge of Kodiak's muzzle.

The dog didn't need to answer the question. Ben knew good and well what Kodiak wanted. He wanted to pull a sled. It was what he'd been born to do. The desire to pull had been bred into him for generations.

Just like me.

Ben was a musher, like his father and his grandfather before him. Mushing was in his blood, whether or not he wanted to admit it. It was more than a sport. It was a life-sustaining instinct, like taking his next breath.

Clementine was right. He'd given up. He was no longer living. Since the loss of his team, his faith had taken more than a hit. It was as if God had vanished, leaving him stranded. Not just out on the Bering Sea, but stranded in life. Nothing was as it was before.

The dog yard was empty, just as it had been since the day of the accident.

Kodiak had spent his first days back at home after that fateful day pacing from one red doghouse to the next, methodically poking his nose in each before swiveling his masked face back toward Ben.

"What happened?" his look seemed to say.

Comforting the distressed dog was impossible, so Ben tried locking him inside the house. That didn't work, either. Kodiak sat on the braided rug by the front door and howled all night. After three sleepless nights listening to the husky's mournful wails, Ben finally relented and let him back outside. He went straight to the dog yard and spent the first night moving silently between the dog boxes. From Ben's vantage point at the cabin window, he looked like a ghost dog floating over the snowdrifts.

He finally settled on top of his doghouse. The wise old owl. He never closed his eyes. It was as if he was standing sentry over the missing.

Ben watched him fight sleep, the dog's furry eyelids drifting closed and then popping back open, until he could no longer stand by and watch. He led Kodiak back inside and tried coaxing him onto the soft new dog bed he'd ordered off the internet. But Kodiak was a sled dog, accustomed to sleeping on a bed of straw. He sniffed at the new bed, walked away and finally slumped into a heap on the wood floor in front of the fireplace.

He slept for two straight days. Ben was so relieved that he'd cried like a baby.

And thus had begun their new life. One where up was down and down was up. One where a sled dog eventually learned to sleep on a puffy dog bed and the musher became a journalist.

His first day of work as a photographer had been a disaster. Barely healed from the frostbite, his hands were so swollen and numb he could scarcely hold the camera, much less reliably press the shutter button. When the office sent him out to take photos of the ribbon-cutting ceremony at the new courthouse, he came back with nothing more than a series of blurred images. The *Yukon Reporter* ran one of them anyway. It was only then that Ben realized he'd been given the job out of pity. Aurora's way of taking care of its own. He'd nearly quit. In the end, he'd decided staying at the *Reporter* was better than sitting in his cabin overlooking the graveyard of doghouses. So he stayed and eventually became an excellent photographer.

Ben inhaled a steadying breath. He couldn't live with those empty doghouses anymore. He pushed thoughts of racing again out of his mind. The prospect of crossing the Bering Sea was too much to handle right now. But climbing on a sled and following his dog into the wilderness was not. In fact, it sounded like perfection. And isn't that what training for a race really was? Taking one day at a time? Mushing a few miles here and there?

He shot off the sofa so fast that Kodiak let loose with a sharp bark. Ben's mind was made up. And now that it was, the urge to get out there on a sled ran deep. He was finally allowing himself to feel it, down in his bones. The desire had always been there, like a persistent itch. He'd simply trained himself to ignore it. It had become more and more difficult to resist since he took Clementine mushing.

She would be busy working on her research notes for the magazine all day. All caught up on work for the time being, Ben had the morning free. Ben figured he could run by Reggie's house, pick up a couple of dogs and be on the sled in less than an hour or two. Maybe he could even take Moose along and see if the stray had any experience with a sled. His old team had been comprised solely of rescue dogs. Giving homeless dogs new meaning had always been one of his favorite things about mushing. There was a certain poetic beauty about starting a new team the same way.

"Kodiak, come on, boy."

The woods and the crisp winter morning were beckoning Ben. And thanks to Clementine, he was finally ready to answer the call.

Clementine found it surprisingly difficult to get her research notes emailed to the *Nature World* offices. Ever since Ben had shown up at her door, eager to "borrow" Moose for the day, she'd been distracted beyond belief. Recounting her dog handling experience seemed of little importance compared to the fact that Ben was out there somewhere, mushing a dog team. And he'd taken Moose!

Work that she could normally do in her sleep took hours. It took every ounce of self-control she could muster to stop herself from slamming shut her laptop and heading back to the animal shelter. There were enough dogs there to make up an entire team.

Get a grip on yourself. You're a researcher, not a sled dog trainer.

She forced herself to keep plugging away. After she'd put in a couple of solid hours, she decided an emergency coffee run was in order. She found Anya behind the counter, wiping it down.

"Hi." She gestured to one of the bar stools. "Have a seat."

"Thanks." Clementine glanced at the chalkboard next to the register, where the Special of the Day was always advertised. "Dark chocolate decadence latte. I have to ask, where in the world do you come up with these drinks?"

Anya shrugged, but there was a glimmer of satisfaction in her eyes. "It's a special skill I have, I suppose. Would you like one?"

"Do you really have to ask?"

"One dark chocolate decadence latte, with extra whipped cream, coming right up." Anya flipped the lever on the espresso machine. It came to life with a hiss.

Clementine sighed. "I could sit right here on this bar stool forever and die happy one day."

"Could you really?" Anya gave her a sideways glance. "I see what's going on here."

Clementine tore her gaze from the picture window, where she could see one of those cute ski planes coming in for a landing, and watched Anya add a layer of steamed milk to her cup. "What do you mean?"

Anya shook the can of whipped topping and raised one accusatory eyebrow. "You've fallen in love."

Clementine nearly fell off her bar stool. She was forced to grip the edge of the counter for support.

Were her feelings for Ben that noticeable? And were they strong enough to be called *love?*

"Um, well, I don't know if I'd go that far," she stammered.

Anya slid an overflowing latte cup across the counter toward her. The contents did indeed smell decadent. "You can't fool me. You've fallen in love with Alaska."

"With Alaska?" Clementine resumed normal breathing. She hadn't even realized she'd stopped. "Oh."

"Oh?" Anya echoed. "What, or should I say who, did you think I meant?"

Clementine dived into her latte so she would have a good excuse not to answer. Anya watched her with interest.

When she could no longer gulp any more of the rich coffee—decadent was an understatement—she put the cup down. "Never mind what I thought you meant. You're one-hundred-percent correct. I am in love with Alaska."

"I knew it. It happens." Anya grinned. "A lot."

"What's it like to really live here?"

"Cold."

Clementine laughed and looked out the window

once more, where the snow had begun to fall in earnest. "I gathered that."

"No, really." Anya nodded toward the window. "This is nothing. It snows here nine months out of the year. Do you think you could grow accustomed to living somewhere like that coming from Texas?"

Clementine bit her lip to stop herself from blurting out *Yes, yes I could!* Why were they even having this conversation? One minute she was ordering coffee, and the next she was talking about moving to Alaska.

"It's really beautiful in the summertime, though. You'd love it," Anya continued, oblivious to the crazy thoughts swirling in Clementine's mind.

"What about the bears?" Clementine glanced at the stuffed grizzly bear standing sentry over the coffee bar. His teeth were awfully pointed. And big.

Anya waved her dish towel at the grizzly. Its fur rippled slightly. "Don't worry about them. It's not as if they're romping up and down the sidewalks. You just have to be careful out in the woods."

Clementine's thoughts turned to the woods by Ben's cabin, which seemed like the perfect place for a bear. She closed her eyes and pictured him there right now, mushing with Kodiak and Moose pulling him through the snow.

"You know—" Anya's voice brought her back to the present "—I could see you living here."

"Really?" Clementine swelled with pride. Hadn't it been only a matter of days since everyone in

Alaska seemed to think she wasn't cut out for much more than making foot lotion?

"Really." Anya nodded. "I can't quite put my finger on it. You just seem to belong here, like you're one of us."

It was probably the nicest thing she could have said.

Upon her return, Clementine heard the barking coming from her room the moment she stepped off the elevator. Her first thought was that at least Nugget hadn't managed to escape while she'd been chatting with Anya, even though the Pomeranian was clearly making her annoyance at being left behind known. Clementine quickened her steps, eager to put an end to the commotion. Yet before she even slid her key card into the lock, she realized the barking didn't sound at all like Nugget's high-pitched little yap.

Woof woof woof.

Pause.

Woof woof woof.

It continued in perfect rhythm, and Clementine realized it wasn't a dog at all. She pushed open the door and spotted her cell phone, with its barking ring tone, vibrating like mad in a wild dance across the dresser. How could she have forgotten to bring her cell phone with her to the coffee bar? Clearly she was more distracted than she even realized.

Nugget didn't pay a bit of attention to the barking

phone. Instead, she took a flying leap from the bed straight into Clementine's arms. Clementine said a silent prayer of thanks when she managed to reach the phone before it stopped barking. She clutched Nugget to her chest and prayed once more—this time that the voice on the other end of the phone would be Ben. It had been only a matter of hours since he'd surprised her by picking up Moose and announcing he was going to take the dog mushing. He was most likely still following the woodland trail that snaked through the forest behind his lovely cabin. She couldn't wait to hear how the morning had gone.

"Hello?" She sounded breathless, eager, but she just couldn't help it.

Natalie began speaking almost before Clementine could even get the word out. "Oh. My. Gosh. The whole office just watched you on TV."

"What?"

Natalie let out a squeal that Clementine was certain could be heard ten cubicles away. "You were on the *Nature World* Channel. As big as life, right there in the office lobby."

Clementine could scarcely believe it. She'd been so wrapped up in helping Reggie get his team to the starting line that she'd forgotten all about the cameraman from *Nature World.* More than that, she'd been thinking about Ben and how he'd once stood beneath the Gold Rush Trail start banner himself.

"So you're still coming back in a few days, right?" Natalie whispered into the phone.

It was a surprising question. Clementine could easily see the printed dates and times of her return trip on the itinerary that was folded neatly in the side pocket of her carry-on bag. But Reggie's parting words rang in her consciousness.

In his heart a man plans his course, but the Lord determines his steps.

Then she remembered what Anya had said only a half hour before.

You've fallen in love...with Alaska.

She swallowed. Hard. "Nat, why are you asking me that?"

"I don't know. I guess because you look so happy there."

"I *am* happy." Clementine's cheeks burned with enough warmth to melt an igloo. "I'm actually thinking about staying a few extra days."

"Really?" Natalie didn't sound at all surprised.

"I'd like to go to Nome for the end of the race." Even as she said the words, Clementine knew her reasons for traveling to Nome had little to do with the race. She wanted a little more time with Ben before she had to say goodbye.

"Well, keep me posted. And don't worry about a thing back here. I've got our cubicle under control."

Natalie transferred Clementine to their supervisor's line, and he quickly gave her approval to travel to Nome. In fact, he seemed to think it was a brilliant idea. Clementine hung up and stroked Nugget, who'd curled up in her lap with the moose dog toy planted firmly in her little jaws. She shook her head and caught the Pomeranian's gaze. "We're going to Nome."

Nugget cocked her head and swiveled her tiny ears, perfect little triangles.

"When Jesus said He wanted me to have a full life, He wasn't kidding."

Nugget yipped in agreement and Clementine buried her face in the dog's fuzzy coat. She'd taken God's Word literally and He'd proven faithful. When she thought of all that had happened since she set foot in Alaska, her head spun. Learning to handle sled dogs, the start of the race, seeing Nugget on the front page of the paper, appearing on TV—the *Nature World* Channel! As miraculous as all of it had been, each one of those events paled in comparison to the moment her feet slid out from under her and she found herself in Ben Grayson's arms. She wasn't going to Nome just to see the end of the race. She was simply prolonging her inevitable trip back home.

I'm falling in love with him.

She lived over three thousand miles away, and she was falling in love with him. Just as she'd fallen in love with Alaska.

She'd come here to find her life, but instead she'd found love. Could Ben Grayson from Aurora,

Alaska, really be the man God intended for her? Was it even possible?

A knock on the door to her room brought an abrupt end to the thought. Clementine hopped off the bed, scooped Nugget in her arms and swung open the door, fully expecting to find Ben standing on the threshold.

She blinked in confusion when instead she found Sue on the other side of the door. Her smile was grim. "Hi, Clementine."

"Hi." Clementine's throat grew dry. Something was wrong. She could feel it. She looked past Sue in search of Ben. But he wasn't there.

Sue's smile grew warmer, but her eyes, black as ravens, remained serious. "I just came from the Gold Rush Trail veterinary office. There's been an accident."

Clementine moved without thinking, setting Nugget on the bed and shoving her arms into her parka. Her mind spun with all the possibilities of what could go wrong out on the trail. If one of Reggie's dogs was simply tired or not feeling well, Sue wouldn't have made an effort to come to the hotel and find her.

Her hands shook as she pulled on her mittens. All she could think about was Ben's description of his dogs disappearing, one by one, under the ice. *Not again. Please, not again.* "Something happened to one of Reggie's dogs, didn't it? We need to find Ben. He'll want to be there for Reggie."

"Not one of Reggie's dogs. One of Ben's." Sue

reached out and touched her arm. "The accident didn't happen on the race trail."

"I don't understand." Clementine shook her head, as if she could shake the past few minutes from her memory. As if Sue had never knocked on her door, and her biggest worry was getting her research notes emailed back to the office before it closed.

Then Sue spoke the words that threatened to break Clementine's heart. "It's Kodiak."

Chapter Fifteen

Ben sat with his head in his hands and tried to figure out how he'd ended up at the Gold Rush Trail veterinary office. Everything that happened this morning was little more than a blur. The one thing he remembered with absolute clarity was Kodiak's bloodcurdling scream, echoing through the forest. It was the worst sound he'd ever heard. More frightening even than the cracking of ice, a sound that would forever make him ill.

He'd known it was Kodiak at once. Even though Kodiak was way ahead of the sled, running lead, there'd been no doubt it was him. Ben knew Kodiak as well as he knew himself. He knew the husky liked to turn eight precise circles before settling down in his bed. He knew that if Kodiak were to lose a booty on the trail, it would be the one on his right hind foot. And when he drank water he always picked out any loose pieces of straw floating on the surface before he took his first sip.

They were connected. They'd been connected before the accident on the Bering Sea, but afterward that bond had grown even deeper. Ben wouldn't have been surprised to find out that when Kodiak bled, he bled, too.

This, as it turned out, wasn't the case.

As the dog's screams bounced off the canopy of snow-laden evergreens, Ben had gone into a sort of trance. Operating on autopilot, he threw the ice hook, stopping the dogs in their tracks. He ran through the shin-deep snow until he reached Kodiak, lying on his side. The dog's breath came in shallow puffs, and the scream had turned into a pathetic whimper. The white snow around him had turned crimson with blood. There wasn't a drop of it on Ben, though.

The dog had stepped on a trap. Its metal jaws were clamped around his left front foot.

Rage had blackened Ben's vision as he'd scooped Kodiak in his arms and carried him back to the sled. He'd been running the dogs on his own property. Whoever had set the trap had done so illegally. It was rusty, meaning it had been there for quite some time. The trapper had likely tried to take advantage of the fact that Ben no longer mushed. When he'd been a contender, he knew the trail around his cabin like the back of his hand.

Ben didn't care who had done it. All he'd cared about was getting help for Kodiak. In his confused daze, he'd taken his dog where he'd always gone for help in his mushing days—to the Gold Rush Trail vet offices. It seemed only natural.

He blinked, trying to remember who had been there when he'd carried a semiconscious Kodiak through the door. He couldn't recall all the familiar faces. He'd just been so relieved to see Dr. Stu Foster, the Gold Rush Trail lead vet. If anyone could fix Kodiak, it was Stu. And Stu, good man that he was, never once had asked Ben why he'd brought Kodiak to the race offices. He'd simply taken the dog from his arms and gone to work.

"Ben?"

Ben looked up and fought back nausea at the sight of blood all over Stu's scrubs.

Kodiak's blood.

"Stu? How is he?" Ben started to stand, but then thought better of it. He didn't trust his knees not to buckle.

"He's going to be fine. He's lost a lot of blood, but we've given him a transfusion. I want to keep him here overnight. He'll need antibiotics and lots of rest, but he's going to be fine, Ben." Stu clamped a comforting hand on Ben's shoulder.

"And his paw…" Ben couldn't bring himself to finish the question. He knew dogs survived with three legs all the time, but a sled dog with a missing limb was too heartbreaking to even contemplate.

"We were able to save it." Stu crossed his arms. Beneath the bill of his Gold Rush Trail baseball cap, the look in the veterinarian's eyes hardened. He spoke sternly, carefully. "Ben, I'm telling you that Kodiak is going to be fine. This isn't like last time. Do you understand?"

Ben nodded.

Not like last time.

He tried to digest the words, to believe them. As they sunk in, he had to fight the flow of relieved tears that threatened to wrack his body. He sniffed and pinched his eyes.

When he was finally able to speak, he managed to choke out, "Thank you. Thank you so much. I know I should have taken him to a regular vet."

"Don't be ridiculous. This is where Kodiak belongs." Stu aimed his finger at Ben's chest. "This is where you belong. Don't forget it."

Ben couldn't even think about such things. Not now. Not when his shirt was still covered with Kodiak's blood from where he'd carried the bleeding dog inside. "I've got to get to Nome tomorrow to cover the end of the race. Can I leave Kodiak here while I'm gone?"

"Absolutely. He needs his rest. We'll take good care of him." Stu nodded toward Moose, curled at Ben's feet. Until that moment, Ben had forgotten about the dog entirely. "Sue said she'd go by your place and pick up Reggie's dogs. She'll get them back home. What about your other dog?"

Ben stared down at Moose. He couldn't even remember bringing the husky with him to the clinic. She was a good dog. He'd actually been surprised the stray dog was so biddable, seeing as she'd been living on the streets. In his experience, it sometimes took a while for stray huskies to come around and trust people. Not that he could blame them.

Biddable or not, Ben was in no condition to even contemplate forming a dog team. "This isn't my dog."

"No?"

"No." Even as Ben denied ownership of the dog, the husky sighed and planted her chin on his foot. She gazed up at him with her mismatched eyes. One blue, one brown.

"Looks like your dog to me." Stu shrugged. "Give me about a half hour or so and then you can come on back and see Kodiak. Don't forget what I said. You belong here, Ben."

Ben said a silent prayer of thanks when Stu disappeared without any further commentary about where he belonged. Ben just couldn't take it anymore. He felt hollowed out, like an empty shell.

Everyone thought he belonged on the trail. He'd never been tempted to listen to anyone's opinion on the matter, save for one. Clementine's opinion mattered to him more than any of the others. He cared about what she thought. He'd wanted to be strong again, for her.

And look where that got me, he thought bitterly. Here.

He should have known better than to think he could mush again. He hadn't entertained the thought in four years. Why had he tried to become a different man now after all this time?

The door to the clinic blew open and Clementine rushed in. Her windswept golden curls framed her flushed face like a halo. She looked innocent, just as she had the first time Ben laid eyes on her.

A bittersweet sadness came over him as he looked at her now. Her beautiful green eyes swam behind a veil of tears.

For love, he realized, and a lonely ache settled in his heart. *I wanted to be a better man because I love her.*

Clementine took a cautious step toward Ben. The glazed, empty look on his face tightened the guilty knot in her stomach. The moment Sue told her that Kodiak had stepped in a trap, remorse had hit Clementine like a slap in the face.

She'd pressured him back on the sled. He'd mushed for the first time in four years with her because she wanted to learn. And then she'd teased him about ending up on a motorcycle with flames. She'd just wanted him to live again, but instead she'd led him here, to this moment. What she wouldn't give to see him driving down Main Street in downtown Aurora on a motorcycle with the biggest, reddest flames imaginable right now.

This is my fault.

She wished he would stand, so she could pull him into a hug. He didn't. He remained sitting on the

bench that lined the wall of the wood-paneled waiting room, with Moose stretched out beneath him.
When Moose trained her mismatched eyes on Clementine, the dog's plumed tail beat a happy rhythm on
the tile floor. She didn't move, though. She remained
right beneath Ben, with her chin resting on the toe
of his shoe, as though standing guard over him.

Fiercely loyal to her musher.

Already.

Clementine blinked furiously in an effort to hold
back her tears and sank onto the bench next to Ben.

"I'm so sorry, Ben." She reached for his hand.
It was icy cold as usual. Clementine wanted nothing more than to warm him up and somehow make
everything better.

"How did you know I was here?" Realization
dawned in his empty eyes and he nodded slowly.
"Sue."

"She came by the hotel and told me about Kodiak."
Clementine was almost afraid to say the dog's name.

She held her breath until Ben released a long sigh.
"He's going to be okay. At least that's what the vet
says. I haven't been able to go back and see him
yet, though."

Clementine finally allowed herself to inhale a
lungful of air. *Thank You, God.* "What happened?"

"His foot got caught in a hunting trap." Ben
clenched his jaw and stared down at the floor. Sure
signs he didn't care to elaborate any further.

Clementine wrapped her fingers around his strong

arm and squeezed, forcing him to look at her. At first he didn't move. He stayed completely still for a long, quiet moment. When at last he turned his gaze on her, his blue eyes were filled with such haunting vulnerability that a deep ache formed in Clementine's chest. She felt as though she could see straight into his soul. And what she saw there was fear.

This was Ben. Her big, rugged Alaskan. The look of raw helplessness on his face was too much.

She gave his arm a squeeze. "He's going to be fine. The vets here for the race are the best in the world."

"I know." Ben hung his head. Despite the good prognosis, he looked as though he carried the weight of the world on his shoulders. "I have to leave for Nome tomorrow for the paper. Kodiak's going to stay here so they can keep an eye on him."

Nome.

Clementine had been so anxious to tell Ben that she, too, would be going there for the end of the race. Now, for some reason, she was afraid. She wished they had more time, that she could wait and tell him later, when he felt better about Kodiak. But time was the one thing they didn't have.

"I'm going, too," Clementine whispered, "to Nome."

Since the moment he'd first kissed her and she saw stars, Clementine knew she had to stay for the end of the race. She knew Ben wanted her there, too. She'd seen it in his eyes at the banquet when he asked her how long they had until she went home.

Even back when they'd gone shopping for her bunny boots, he'd wistfully told her how much she would love Nome.

But his reaction now was one of cold, stony silence. He was so quiet, in fact, that Clementine wondered if he'd even heard what she said.

"I'm going to Nome," she repeated and made her best attempt at a smile.

If Clementine had held out any hope that he would still be happy at the news, it vanished when she heard him speak.

"I heard you the first time," he said flatly.

He didn't sound angry at all. In fact, Clementine would have preferred that he did. Instead, he sounded empty. Dead inside. And she knew without a doubt that the fear she'd seen in his eyes had made its way straight to his heart and squeezed it in a vise so tight there was no longer room for anything—or anyone—else.

Whatever had developed between the two of them had vanished. However beautiful it had been, it had lasted only an instant, like diamond dust.

She took a deep, steadying breath. It might be too late for her and Ben, but she wasn't about to leave for Texas, Nome or anywhere else without making sure he didn't blame himself for another four years.

Shame coursed through her. She shouldn't have encouraged him to mush again. He'd said taking her had been a one-time thing, and she should have left it at that. Why did she have to ask him if he missed it? Ben led a perfectly respectable life. She couldn't imagine the pain he'd lived through the last time he attempted to conquer the Gold Rush Trail. He'd obviously been working on his relationship with God. She wished she'd been more patient. It might be obvious to her—and most everyone else in Ben's life— that he was meant to return to mushing, but it was a dangerous sport. Only Ben would know when he was ready.

"Ben, what happened to Kodiak today wasn't your fault. If anyone should feel responsible, it's me."

"No." He shook his head. "Don't say that."

"I pressured you. You wouldn't have been out there if I hadn't come to Alaska." She swallowed around the quickly expanding lump in her throat. "I should have minded my own business."

"Stop," he ground out through clenched teeth. "Please."

He lifted his hand to her face and traced the curve of her jaw with his fingertip. "Don't you see? Your sense of adventure, your thirst for life…it's one of the things I love most about you."

Clementine wished she could put her finger to his lips and stop him from saying anything else.

"You challenge me." He smiled a bittersweet smile and dropped his hand back to his lap. "I thought I could be man enough to live up to that challenge, but I can't. I tried. It's hard. You can't imagine how hard."

"Ben," she started to protest, but he gave her a weary look that said she may as well not bother.

"I think it would be best if you didn't go to Nome," he said calmly.

"I understand." Clementine stood and wrapped her arms around herself. Her teeth chattered and she suddenly felt colder than she had since the moment she first set foot in Alaska.

Ben rose to his feet and wrapped his arms around her. His embrace, which had once felt like home, now felt like nothing more than a goodbye.

"Bye, Ben." She backed out of his arms, eager to escape to the refuge of her hotel room and figure out what to do next. Where to go. He'd made it clear he didn't want her in Nome. But going back to Texas now seemed utterly out of the question.

"Wait." Ben grabbed her wrist.

She stopped and searched his face for a sign that he'd come to his senses and made room for her, and God, in his heart again. She found none. "Yes?"

He glanced down at Moose but didn't say anything.

He didn't have to.

Clementine called the dog to her side and the two of them walked out the door without a backward glance.

Chapter Sixteen

Next to walking away from Ben, returning Moose to the animal shelter was the hardest thing Clementine had ever done. What normally would have been difficult beyond measure was made even worse by the tender state of her emotions. She stood before the reception desk trembling, with tears in her eyes, as the poor dog leaned into her side. In the end, she couldn't even manage to look Moose in the eye before she fled the building and made a beeline back to the Northern Lights Inn.

At least she'd stayed long enough to make sure the shelter staff knew Moose's name. The husky would no longer be a nameless, homeless dog. Every living creature deserved a name.

By the time Clementine stumbled through the revolving door of the hotel, she wanted nothing more than to crawl in bed and pull the covers over her head. She forced herself to pack first, figuring she may as well get that over with, too. Next, she finished emailing her notes to the office. Then she lay in bed and stared at the ceiling of her darkened hotel room. Sleep was impossible.

In less than twelve hours she would be on a flight home. Beside her, Nugget was curled into a tight ball, with her tail wrapped around her tiny black nose. *Like a miniature little sled dog,* Clementine realized with a pang.

"I didn't realize you would take that T-shirt so literally," she murmured. The puff of fur on Nugget's head moved with Clementine's breath and tickled her chin.

She wondered how long the Pomeranian would sleep in such a position after they returned to Texas. How many nights would it take before she stretched out on her back with her paws in the air like she had before? One? Three? Ten?

Likewise, how many nights would it take for Clementine to forget the feel of snow flurries falling on her skin? How many days would pass before she once again felt more at home sitting in her *Nature World* cubicle than standing on a sled zipping through a forest of evergreens?

And how long before she stopped missing Ben?

She glanced at her bags, packed and piled beside the door. Disguised by the shadows of the unlit room, they could have belonged to anyone, headed anywhere. Texas, Fairbanks…Nome.

It wasn't too late to change her mind. She'd never changed her plane ticket. Even though the one in her handbag had Houston, Texas, as its destination, there were still a handful of seats available on the evening flight to Nome. She'd checked one last time just before climbing into bed. If she booked a reservation, she would no longer be on the same afternoon flight as Ben, but she'd be there by midnight.

Her fingers itched, anxious to redial the number for the airline. She knew the phone number by heart.

But Ben didn't want her. In Nome. Or anywhere. He'd said so himself.

Deep down, Clementine hoped it had only been his grief talking. Kodiak stepping in the trap had taken Ben back to a time and place he'd barely begun to leave in the past. Once he had time to heal, he might regret telling her to leave.

But when would that healing come? Four years had passed since the first accident and his wounds were still as fresh as new fallen snow.

She couldn't throw herself at Ben when he'd asked her to leave. Doing so would go against every safe, carefully planned move she'd ever made. She belonged back in Texas. At home she had a nice condo and a good—albeit boring at times—job. Her parents were there. And she belonged to a good church, the same one where she'd attended Sunday school as a little girl. Her friends were there. Her life was there.

Her safe, predictable life.

She let her eyelids drift closed. As she did, the

words that never failed to bring her comfort came to her lips. She spoke them aloud.

I have come that they may have life, and have it to the full.

The verse had become seared into her consciousness. She'd thought she was ready to claim such a promise—even on that first day, when she'd fallen into Ben's arms on the icy pavement. She hadn't realized just how full her life could become. All she had to do now was take that last step.

All she had to do was go to Nome and tell Ben she was in love with him.

Lord, what should I do?

Her answer came in a gentle whisper.

I have come that you *may have life, and have it to the full.*

At first, Clementine failed to notice the subtle difference.

The whisper grew louder.

You *may have life.*

Goose bumps pricked her arms. The verse was meant for her. Not just everyone, a collective mass of people. It was a promise to her, directly from her Savior.

She hadn't really thought of it in quite such an intimate way before. Going to Nome and facing Ben again frightened the life out of her.

Then she thought of Ben mushing again. He'd taken a chance. Wasn't it time for her to take a chance, too?

What if he really meant what he said? What if he didn't love her back?

She knew what would happen if that were the case. God would heal her heart. But if she never gave Ben a chance, she would always wonder…*what if?*

She couldn't go back home. Not yet.

Home.

As she turned the word over in her mind, Clementine realized she already felt at home. Alaska was home. She wanted to live in a place where the air sparkled with diamonds and build a life with the man whose kiss put them there.

She threw off the covers and flicked on the bedside lamp, flooding the room with light. Nugget squinted at the sudden brightness before poking her nose under Clementine's pillow.

"Sorry, sleepyhead," she cooed. "Although I don't know how you can sleep at a time like this."

Her fingers flew over the number keys on her cell phone so fast that she misdialed three times. When at last she reached Alaska Airlines, a computerized voice told her she had a seven-minute wait before she could speak to a representative.

Each passing second seemed like a lifetime. The annoying hold music only made the time pass even slower. When the third song got under way, Nugget popped her head out from beneath the pillows and swiveled her fuzzy head toward the door.

She curled her tiny lip and growled.

Clementine frowned. She, too, felt like growling. Was a ticket agent ever going to pick up the line?

Nugget hopped off the bed and scurried to the door. She sniffed at the crack at the bottom and the sliver of light shining in from the hallway, growled again and yipped impatiently at Clementine.

"Nugget, not now. Okay?"

Not one to be ignored, the little dog spun a quick circle and barked once more.

Her bark was followed by a soft knock at the door. Clementine's heart jumped to her throat and she nearly dropped the phone.

Ben?

Nugget barked yet again and scratched at the door.

Clementine propelled herself into action. Being careful not to disconnect her call, she wedged the phone between her ear and her shoulder and scooped Nugget into her arms.

She swung the door open without even checking the peephole, certain that she would find Ben on the other side. Instead, Bob Easton, the hotel manager, stood in the doorway holding a large, white gift box.

"Hi." Clementine nodded toward Nugget squirming in her arms. "I know you're not here to tell me you found my dog again. She's safe with me, at least for the time being."

"I'm not here about Nugget." He grinned and held the gift box toward her. "This was delivered this morning, to your attention. I tried to catch you when you came in earlier, but you seemed upset. I didn't want to bother you."

"Oh." Clementine glanced at the box. "I'm sorry. It's been kind of a rough day."

"Well, maybe this will help. It looks as though it could be something special." Bob stepped one foot inside the room and slid the box onto the dresser.

"Thank you."

She waited until the door was safely clicked shut before releasing Nugget. Then she turned her attention toward the mysterious box. It was a rectangular, white box tied with a red silky bow. Clementine bent to inspect the package and found her name written on a large envelope, fixed in place beneath the bow's smooth satin ribbon.

Her breath caught in her throat.

Ben?

Of course. Who else would send her a gift?

She clicked the phone's speaker button and set it on the dresser. Nugget let out a dramatic yawn and hopped back in bed.

Clementine's hands trembled with anticipation as she pulled the ribbon loose. She ran her fingers over the handwriting that spelled out her name and broke the envelope's seal. She slid the contents into her lap.

It was a stack of 5 x 7 photographs, neatly bound with a rubber band. She let her gaze fall on the picture on top. It was from her first full day in Alaska—the day she'd built the snowman. In it, her hair whipped around in the wind, but even her wild curls couldn't hide her expression of sheer delight as she patted snow into place on the top layer of the snowman. Nugget had jumped clear off the ground and looked as though she were suspended in midair, with her pink booties dangling from her dainty paws.

The next photograph had been taken at her dog handling class and showed Clementine with the cream-colored husky she'd been assigned to handle. She was holding on to the dog's purple harness and running alongside the gang line. Clementine had no idea when Ben had taken the photo. When he'd come to check on her after the ambulance had pulled into the parking lot, he hadn't had his camera. He must have gone back to get it and snapped the picture after class had resumed. She smiled at the image of Akiak. With his tongue hanging out of the side of his mouth, he looked so happy and free. And when she let her gaze fall on her own image, Clementine couldn't help but think she, too, looked brave.

"Akiak," she whispered.

And a shiver of awareness ran through her as she remembered Ben telling her the same thing on that very day.

There were more photographs, about ten in all. From the image of her gazing awestruck at the ice sculptures in the park to the photo of her first time standing on the runners of a sled, Clementine barely recognized herself. Each picture was more mesmerizing than the last.

And together, they told a story. The story of a woman who'd come thousands of miles in search of something and, by the looks of things, she'd found it.

With great care, she restacked the photographs, slid them back into their envelope and turned her attention to the box.

Her heart hammered as she lifted the smooth white lid and peeled back layer upon layer of wisp-thin tissue paper. What she found buried beneath them took her breath away. Nestled inside was the sapphire velvet parka she'd tried on at the Gold Rush Trail banquet.

She blinked in disbelief. Surely this wasn't the same coat.

She ran her fingers over the luxurious velvet and then let them skim the soft silver fur of the collar.

It was most definitely the same coat.

She lifted it from the box. As she did, a slip of white paper fluttered to the floor. Clementine slipped her arms in the sleeves of the parka and lifted the hood until the fur tickled her nose. Then she bent to examine Ben's note, only to find it wasn't a note at all.

Rather, she found herself holding a plane ticket for the evening flight from Aurora to Nome.

"Alaska Airlines. May I help you?"

Clementine tore her gaze from the treasure in her hand and searched out her cell phone, still switched to the speaker phone setting on the nightstand.

A tiny voice called out, "Hello?"

Clementine clutched the plane ticket to her heart and spoke into the phone. Even she could hear the smile in her voice. "Hi. I'm so sorry, but I won't need any help after all."

"There's nothing I can do for you today?"

"No, thank you." She was sure Ben had arranged for the box to be delivered before Kodiak's injury. Afterward, there simply hadn't been time. She decided it didn't matter. Ben wanted her to go to Nome. Somewhere, deep inside, she prayed he still did. "I have everything I need."

Watching Clementine walk away from him was the worst sort of torture Ben could have imagined. It was a wonder he could still breathe by the time she disappeared through the double glass doors of the veterinary clinic.

She hadn't looked back. Not once.

But even through the swirl of fresh snow flurries on the other side of the doors, he'd seen the shake of her shoulders and knew she was crying. He'd felt unworthy, down to his center. It was a feeling that tortured him throughout the night, worse than any nightmares he'd ever had of the trail. How could he have told her to go back to Texas when she'd been willing to extend her trip and come with him to Nome? Sitting in that waiting room, covered with Kodiak's blood, he'd convinced himself he was doing Clementine a favor. She deserved a real man.

A whole man. Not one who'd been so beaten down by circumstances that he was afraid to live the life God had given him.

Lying in the dark, he knew the truth—he hadn't done Clementine a favor. He'd broken her heart.

And perhaps worse, he'd sent Moose away with her. In the end, she couldn't even count on him to give the poor dog a home. He wouldn't be a bit surprised if she despised him now.

Morning came, slow, painful and lonely. On the way to the airport, Ben stopped at the animal shelter, hoping he wouldn't find Moose there. Maybe Clementine had decided to ignore his outburst and go to Nome after all. It certainly wouldn't be the first time she'd ignored his opinion on matters.

When he found Moose pouting in the corner of one of the kennels, he gave up whatever last shred of hope remained. Clementine would never take Moose back to the shelter if she planned on staying in Alaska. She was probably already gone.

Ben wiggled his fingers through the chain link of the kennel enclosure. "Come on, bud. I'm sure you'd prefer her, but it looks as though you're stuck with me."

Moose bounded toward him and licked his cheek through the fence, indicating all was forgiven. The dog's unfailing loyalty made Ben feel even worse, if that was possible. After spending a lifetime with dogs, he hadn't learned a thing about faithfulness. How was that possible?

Shame settled in his gut like a lead weight as he made his way to the shelter lobby and told the receptionist he was ready to adopt Moose. She didn't seem at all surprised at his request, and he couldn't help but wonder if Clementine had told her that he might come for the dog. Maybe she hadn't given up on him after all. Since day one, she'd had more faith in him than he did in himself.

It didn't matter. She was gone. And he'd been the one who sent her away.

Despite the realization that he'd likely never see her again, his thoughts snagged on the word *faith*.

Faith.

Perhaps it played more of a part in what he'd done than he realized. Not faith in himself, but rather, faith in the Lord.

He couldn't shake the regret that followed him as he boarded the plane at the airport. With Moose safely tucked away in the cargo section of the aircraft, and Stu's assurances via phone that Kodiak was resting peacefully, Ben thought he might find a glimmer of peace in his soul as he headed toward Nome. But the question of faith nagged at him and refused to let him go as he arrived in the place where he'd once thought Clementine would join him.

He went through the motions of retrieving Moose from the tiny baggage section of the Nome airport and getting the keys to his rental car. When he found the SUV in the parking lot, beneath a thick layer of snow, he tossed his bags inside and got Moose settled on the passenger seat. Ben crawled in the driver's side and rested his forehead against the steering wheel.

I've lost her and it's all my fault.

"It's not a choice. It's not as if I decided to be this way," he muttered aloud.

Moose, sitting straight up beside him, let out a soft woof and swiveled her pointy husky ears. As Ben watched the dog, a voice floated up somewhere from the depths of his consciousness.

You have a choice now.

Ben wasn't sure where the words came from. God? Clementine? It certainly sounded like something she would say.

He wished it were that easy, that he could simply decide to place all his trust in the Lord.

He let his eyes drift closed. Weariness settled over him, bone-deep. But his physical exhaustion was nothing compared to the ache in his soul. He wondered what it would be like to finally let it all go. To lean on God with everything he had. With a pang, he realized he already knew what it was like. He'd lived that way *before*.

He'd been a regular at church, never doubting for a moment the existence of the Creator. He'd mushed his dog team into some of the most majestic territory on the planet, places that took his breath away. And he'd done so filled not with fear but with awe at the beauty all around him. For a time, he'd been fearless. He'd been a true believer.

Lord, I want to be that man again. Help me get there.

A plane roared overhead, forcing his eyes open.

He'd never be able to hear the Lord's voice. Not here. Not now. He knew where he needed to go.

He shifted the car into Drive and turned out of the parking lot. Darkness had descended on Nome, and the airport vanished from his rearview mirror quickly as he headed toward the light.

Chapter Seventeen

Historic Nome Community Church stood above all the other buildings in the tiny Gold Rush town. Since the early 1900s its tall, slender steeple dominated the skyline, stretching to heaven. Crafted from whitewashed brick, the church and its stunning spire appeared as though they were born from the tundra. Nightfall only made the church more spectacular.

When he pulled up at the church and clicked off the engine in the shadow of the steeple, he felt utterly alone. For once, the company of a dog wasn't enough. He gave Moose an apologetic pet and leaned into the backseat to dig through his duffel bag. Somewhere beneath all of his clothes, he'd tossed in his Bible.

Locating the book hadn't been an easy task. After flipping through the one at the Northern Lights Inn had become a nightly routine, Ben had decided to find his old Bible back at the cabin. It was the last thing he'd done before heading to Reggie's place to return his dogs the day he'd taken Clementine mushing. He'd looked for it on the bookshelf by the fireplace, where he knew it had once occupied a regular spot.

When he didn't find it there, he'd searched the dresser drawers, his closet and finally the old trunk in the living room that served as his coffee table. The fact that he at last unearthed it from the bottom of the trunk, buried beneath old photographs and newspaper accounts of his mushing days, spoke volumes.

But at least he had it.

He'd yet to open it. With everything that had happened, he hadn't had so much as a minute to spare. Now, with Clementine gone and Kodiak recovering in the hospital, the night stretched before him, lonely and endless.

He grabbed the Bible and stalked out of the car, with Moose trailing on his heels. Something about being out in the open appealed to him, as though God would somehow be easier to find. Ridiculous, he knew, especially considering the temperature had dipped well below zero, but he'd reached the point of desperation.

He settled himself on a concrete bench facing the historic building. The bench was cold, cold enough that Ben felt it even through his base layer and insulated ski pants. Thankfully it was dry. With a sigh, Moose curled into a ball at his feet.

Ben fixed his gaze on the church and a flicker of disappointment passed through him. This was the closest he'd been to God's house in years. He'd expected sitting here to feel different somehow. But it didn't. He bowed his head anyway, pushing down his yearning to sense God's nearness.

Lord, forgive me for what I said to Clementine yesterday. Bring her back to me. I can't lose her.

The prayer seemed hollow. Empty. He could only hope it reached God's ear.

He gave it another try.

I love her, Lord. Please give me the chance to tell her.

And I want to make things right between You and me. I just don't know where to start.

What was wrong with him? This all used to be so easy.

An old-fashioned streetlamp bathed the churchyard in a soft, warm glow. Ben spread his Bible open on his lap and squinted at the tiny print. He'd flipped to the nineteenth chapter of the book of Psalms, which seemed as good a place to be as any. The dim light made it a challenge to read, but he was able to make out the words on the page.

"'The heavens declare the glory of God; the skies proclaim the work of his hands. Day after day they pour forth speech; night after night they display knowledge. There is no speech or language where their voice is not heard. Their voice goes out into all the earth, their words to the end of the world.'"

Ben lifted his gaze to the sky, searching for something, anything that would reassure him. All he saw was a vast expanse of black velvet night. If it proclaimed anything, he couldn't understand it. It only made matters worse that Clementine was somewhere in that sky, headed not to Nome, but back to Texas. Over three thousand miles away.

The thought brought a bitter taste to his mouth.

He slammed the Bible shut, stood and wandered away from the light of the streetlamp. He waded through the deep snow of the churchyard, his feet disappearing with every step until he stood at the base of the steeple. The cross at the top looked small and far away from such an angle, and Ben could barely see it. This struck him as profoundly sad. He squeezed his eyes closed.

God, if I can't find You here—really find You—I don't know where else to look.

His heart pounded a furious beat of desperation. He could feel the final threads of his resistance coming loose at last. It scared the life out of him. In that moment, Ben wanted nothing more than to turn around, get back in the car and drive away. But his love for Clementine kept him rooted to the spot. And the aching need he'd carried inside for so long—the need to get his life back—drove him to his knees.

He sank into the snow. He was half-buried and freezing, but he no longer cared. He dropped his head in his hands and cried out, with everything he had.

"Help me, Lord. I want to trust You, but I can't do it on my own. I need Your help. I need You."

The air around him stilled. He lifted his face to heaven, opened his eyes and was filled with a sense of wonder so deep it rocked him to his core. A luminous arch of crystal blue light stretched across the sky. Tiny whispers of pink tinted its edges, reminding him fiercely of Clementine. The colors intensified, rolling like smoke.

Ben couldn't move. All he could do was stare and hope that what he was seeing wasn't a dream.

The blue ribbon of light waved and danced and was quickly joined by a larger fluorescent glow of deep violet. The violet light arced upward before broadening until it fell across the night. A magnificent, shimmering purple veil.

Frigid wind blew across Ben's face, reminding him this was really happening. It wasn't a dream.

"The auroras," he whispered, his voice breaking with emotion.

He'd seen the Northern Lights before, but never like this. They'd always been beautiful, and had been known to come out of nowhere, decorate the sky and disappear in a matter of minutes. But the timing of this display was in no way coincidental. This time the lights seemed to shine just for him.

He watched in awe as more ribbons of light swirled and danced before his eyes. Undulating bands of yellow, orange and dark red appeared, drawn by God's fingers. Each color shined with the fullness of His mercy. The rays bounced off the white walls of the church and the surrounding snow, casting vivid shadows in every direction. Ben was plunged into a kaleidoscope of color.

A sense of utter tranquility washed over him, along with the unwavering knowledge that everything was going to be all right. He was kneeling in a cathedral built by God Himself, the night sky a window of stained glass.

The words of the Psalm he'd read rose in his heart. *The heavens declare the glory of God; the skies proclaim the work of His hands.*

"Thank You," Ben said, with tears gathering in the corners of his eyes. "Thank You, Lord."

He stood and reached a hand toward the sky. He'd never felt so tall, like if he reached high enough, he could touch the faraway cross atop the steeple, glowing faintly gold against the spectacular light of the auroras.

And standing there, beneath the wonder of a sky lit with the promises of his Savior, Ben finally came home.

Clementine tightened her grip on Nugget's dog carrier and made her way off the plane and onto the tarmac where she was hit with a blast of frigid Nome air. She'd been somewhat prepared for the below-freezing temperatures—well, as prepared as a Texas girl could be—but hadn't realized how remote the small Alaskan village was. As the plane had lifted away from Aurora, the city lights were soon replaced with tiny dots of orange far below.

The pilot explained they were small campfires glowing in the bush, the only signs of civilization in the remote areas of Alaska that could only be reached by plane or dog sled. The campfires belonged to the mushers of the Gold Rush Trail who also were making their way to Nome. As the plane climbed higher, the glowing dots of orange had grown even smaller until they disappeared entirely.

Nome itself was nothing more than a small scattering of lights. Clementine felt as though she were stepping off the plane and into another world.

She'd barely crossed the threshold into the tiny airport when she was greeted with a familiar face. "Clementine?"

Relief washed over her when she spotted Sue Chase. She'd felt so alone. Seeing a friend now was just what she needed. "Sue?"

"Hi. I was just here checking on one of Reggie's dropped dogs." Sue's dark eyes twinkled when she spoke of her husband. "I suppose Ben is picking you up?"

Clementine bit her lip. "He doesn't exactly know I'm here."

Sue's smile grew wider. "Well, isn't he in for a nice surprise?"

Her words warmed Clementine's heart. She hoped they were true. "Thank you. Ben's a very special man."

"Reggie and I certainly think so. Can I give you a lift to your hotel?"

"Thank you. I'd like that."

They chatted like old friends on the way to town from the airport. In a way, Clementine felt as if she'd known Sue for years. She told Sue how Reggie had shared the Bible verse with her at the Gold Rush Trail starting line and how it had planted the seed for her to stay in Alaska for the end of the race.

"That's my Reggie." The affection Sue felt for her husband showed in her smile.

Only then did it occur to Clementine how difficult it must be for her, knowing her husband was trekking across the frigid Alaskan wilderness with little more than a sled and a pack of dogs. "I'll bet you miss him when he's out on the trail."

"I do." She nodded. "But he's doing what he loves. Mushing is a part of him, just like Ben. I know he's upset about Kodiak, but I can't tell you how happy I was to hear that he's mushing again. It's been a long time coming."

Clementine stared quietly at her lap.

Sue took a sidelong glance at her. "God will restore Ben's lost years. Have faith." Sue reached over and squeezed her hand. "It will happen."

Clementine let her gaze wander out the window. As if it were putting an exclamation point on Sue's promise, an elegant white steeple rose above the sleepy town of Nome. Its winsome beauty took her breath away.

As they drew closer, Sue pointed to the spire. "That's Nome Community Church. It was built in 1901. Back then, Nome was the biggest city in Alaska." She chuckled. "Hard to believe, right?"

Clementine thought of how tiny the community looked from the window of the plane and was ready to agree, but her attention was suddenly drawn to a lonely figure standing in the churchyard. "Is that…"

Her heart thundered as she clutched Sue's arm and cried, "Wait."

She would have known the powerful set of those shoulders anywhere. The man standing in the dim light of the church's lamp was Ben. And a familiar-looking dog Clementine never thought she'd see again sat by his side.

Moose?

"Oh, my." Sue pulled the car to a stop on the side of the road. "That's Ben, isn't it?"

"Yes. Yes, it is." Clementine was already buttoning her coat and gathering Nugget's dog carrier in her arms.

"What's he doing at the church this time of night?" Sue glanced at her watch. "It's nearly one in the morning."

"I don't know, but would you mind…" Clementine heard the longing in her voice and hoped Sue did as well.

"Of course not. Get out of here. Go to him. Shoo."

Clementine scrambled out the door, but not without first giving Sue a quick hug. "Thank you."

"Don't mention it." She grinned, leaving Clementine with the certainty that the two of them were sure to become close friends. "Stay warm out there. I'll see you tomorrow."

Clementine lifted the fur-trimmed hood of her parka and watched Sue drive away before turning toward Ben. His back was to her and his face was tilted toward the sky. Even from where she stood, she could tell he looked different somehow. She couldn't quite put her finger on it.

Then his face shifted, ever so slightly, and she saw the unmistakable look of peace on his ruggedly beautiful features. She paused to drink in the sight of him looking so calm and serene, the opposite of the way he'd looked when she'd last seen him. It brought her such happiness that her heart clenched.

"Ben?"

He turned, and the look of tranquility on his face was instantly infused with joy. The fact that he seemed happy to see her was not lost on her. "Clementine?"

She nodded. "I'm here. In Nome."

He shook his head in apparent disbelief. "How did you know I was here at the church?"

"I ran into Sue at the airport and I saw you when we drove past. I asked her to drop me here." The impulsiveness of her actions filled her with sudden shyness. "I hope that's okay."

"Of course it's okay. It's more than okay." He held his arms out wide. "Get over here, you."

Her feet crunched through the snow with ever-increasing rapidity until she realized she was running into his arms. She landed in his embrace with her head against his shoulder. He dipped his face toward hers and pressed a kiss against her cheek.

He whispered her name. "Clementine."

He said it again and again. "Clementine, Clementine." It was a lullaby that soothed every worn place in her heart.

"Welcome to Nome," he whispered and smoothed her wayward curls away from her eyes with his free hand.

Although reluctant to leave the shelter of his strong arms, she pulled away slightly to face him. "You brought Moose."

"I sure did. Someone told me recently I was in need of a sled dog." He glanced down at Moose and grinned.

"And Kodiak?"

"Kodiak is doing great. He'll come home as soon as I get back to Aurora."

"Good. I know you told me not to come, but you know how I feel about obeying orders…" she started. But before she could finish he pressed a cold fingertip against her lips to quiet her.

He smiled, his eyes full of tenderness. "I've never been happier to be ignored in all my life."

"I got your package with the pictures and the coat." She spun a quick circle, modeling the parka for him. "And the plane ticket. I had to come. Thank you."

He cradled her face with frigid fingers.

Clementine covered them with her own gloved hands. "Ben, you're freezing. How long have you been out here?"

He laughed. "Long enough for God to finally get through to me."

Such an answer was the only thing that could explain the newfound peace about him. Still, she hesitated to rejoice. She wanted nothing more than for him to come back to the Lord. Come back with his whole heart. The idea that he finally had seemed almost too good to be true. "What happened?"

He ran a hand through his windblown hair. The tips of his ears were bright red. His cheeks and nose, too.

Windburn, Clementine realized with a pang. And suddenly she could picture it, plain as day. Ben in some remote bush village, warming his hands over a campfire, gathering straw for his dogs. Mushing into Nome.

Hope rose in her soul, and she listened to what he had to say.

"I didn't trust Him. Not really." The corner of his mouth turned down. "I'd been praying more. Reading my Bible. But I wasn't ready to let go. I thought it was all up to me, that I could control my life."

It was hard to hear, even though Clementine had known that was how he felt. "None of us are capable of such a thing."

"I know," he whispered. The gravity in his blue

eyes told her it was true. "I came here looking for an answer. At first, I didn't think anything would change. Then I got down on my knees to pray…"

His voice broke, and with it, a tiny piece of Clementine's heart. She pressed a hand against his chest and felt his heart beating furiously within. Strong, steady, with brand-new purpose. "Go on."

"And when I opened my eyes, He showed me." He looked up at the sky and his lips curved into a broad smile. "The auroras were here."

Clementine gasped and followed his gaze. She saw only the same bright scattering of stars she'd seen in Aurora. The Alaskan sky was gorgeous, filled with starlight the likes of which she'd never seen in Texas. But tonight it wasn't stars she was looking for. "The Northern Lights. I missed them?"

"They'll be back, don't worry." He reached her face and ran his thumb in soothing circles over her cheek. "You'll see them someday."

The way he looked at her with such love in his gaze made her yearn for him to stare at her that way forever. Now even more so than before. Now his was a godly love.

She trembled at his touch. His fingers were so cold that she was beginning to worry about them. She took hold of his hand, turned and pulled him to follow her. "We've got to get you inside. You're going to freeze to death."

He pulled against her. "Wait."

"This can't be good for your frostbite." She turned around, ready to drag him to the car. But when she did, it looked as though he had no immediate plans to leave.

He was lowering himself to one knee.

"Ben, really, can't you pray at the hotel?" She gave his hand a gentle tug.

"I'm not kneeling now because I want to pray." With deliberate slowness, he slid the glove away from her hand. He fixed his gaze on hers, brought her hand to his lips and kissed each of her fingertips.

Clementine could only watch as blissful pleasure, such as she'd never known, took root in her soul. Ben paused for a beat, just to look at her, and she was glad. She wanted to capture the moment—a mental picture, one to rival all the countless beautiful images she'd seen in her life.

At last he spoke. "Clementine, sweetheart, will you marry me?"

"Yes." The word bubbled up her throat. She wouldn't have been physically able to say anything else. "I would love nothing more than to marry you."

He stood, wrapped his arms around her and whispered, "I have another important question to ask you."

"Yes?" It was all she could say. Yes, yes, yes.

He drew back and lifted an inquisitive brow. "How would you feel about being a musher's wife?"

"I think I could grow accustomed to that." Her

lips curved into a smile that she doubted would ever go away. "There were so many sled dogs at the shelter. Maybe we could go back for them. I could help you train them for racing."

"Naturally." He pushed the hood of her parka away from her face. The arctic wind whipped through her hair, but she felt comfortably warm. "Do you think the magazine would let you work from Alaska?"

She shook her head. "I'm leaving the magazine. I'm tired of looking at life through photographs. I'm ready to build a real life for myself...for us. Here."

Us. She loved the way it sounded.

"So you want to train sled dogs now?" His grin grew tenfold. "We'll be a team. Husband and wife."

"Good answer," she murmured as his lips came down on hers.

It was a poignant kiss, full of hope and promises. As her lips touched his, Clementine thought she could see their future stretched out before her, as wide and limitless as the Alaskan sky. The kiss left nothing unsaid. Every small movement of his lips told her exactly how much he cherished her. When at last they broke apart, and Clementine's eyes fluttered open, she fully expected to see stars.

Still, the spectacle that greeted her when she lifted her gaze to the sky made her gasp.

She didn't see stars. Not this time. Instead, the sky was awash with brilliant color. Glittering purples and blues, moving and dancing to some unseen rhythm. One that played for a musher and his bride-to-be.

Epilogue

One Year Later

Clementine refilled her tray with foam cups of steaming hot chocolate and grinned at Anya. "Everyone says the hot chocolate is better this year than ever before."

"Don't be silly. Hot chocolate is hot chocolate." Anya waved off the compliment. She'd made the trek from Aurora to Nome for the end of the Gold Rush Trail, as had most everyone in Aurora.

Clementine doubted there was a soul left in the small town. Then again, this year was special. And not just because of Anya's gourmet hot chocolate.

"She's being serious. We're going to run out at this rate." Sue Chase reached for one of the cups and took a sip. "Nothing wrong with a little quality control," she said with a wink.

Sue had recruited Clementine to join the other mushers' wives on the Gold Rush Trail Hospitality

Committee. Clementine was grateful to have something to do while she waited for Ben to cross the finish line. Passing out hot chocolate was a welcome distraction from the butterflies swirling in her stomach. Nome was a bit cold for butterflies, but Clementine had them in droves.

"How are you ladies doing?" Todd Grayson joined them near the burled arch that marked the finish line for the race.

At the sight of her father-in-law, a swell of anticipation rose in Clementine's heart. Ben didn't expect to see his dad in Nome. Both of his parents had been in attendance at the Gold Rush Trail banquet in Aurora, but Ben thought his dad had returned to Florida with his mom once the race began. Having his father witness his first finish since his return to competitive mushing would no doubt mean the world to Ben.

"Hi, Mr. Grayson," Anya chattered out in greeting.

"Are you ready to see your husband cross the finish line?" Todd asked, a proud gleam shining in his eyes. They were the palest, clearest blue. Just like Ben's.

Everyone turned their attention to Clementine.

Her husband. The words never failed to both surprise and delight her at the same time. It had been ten months, almost a year, since she'd walked down the aisle at the little white church just down the street. Down a burgundy carpet, lined with family and friends, toward the man she thanked God for every day.

She'd missed him while he'd been gone. More than once, she'd been tempted to climb aboard one of the tiny planes headed for various checkpoints along the trail so she could see him. She needed to touch his face, check his hands for signs of frostbite and make sure he was safe. If Sue and Anya hadn't been there to stop her, she just might have gone.

It was a good thing her friends had been stubborn in their determination to make Clementine keep her promise to stay and wait for him in Nome. The trail was filled with enough danger, not to mention the ghosts of Ben's past that Clementine knew still haunted him occasionally. He needed a clear head when he led his team over the frozen trail to the burled arch.

It was her fierce love for her husband that prompted her to stay behind and let him finish his race. In the past seven days, she'd held hands with Sue and prayed for Ben and Reggie. As mushers' wives, they shared a common bond. Clementine had been there, watching, when Reggie arrived in Nome safely only hours before. And now Sue was here, offering the same support to Clementine.

Tears stung the corner of Clementine's eyes. She blinked them back and looked at all the anxious faces, waiting for her to say something.

"Of course she's ready to see Ben." Anya waved

a mittened hand in her direction. "Look at her. She's a mess."

Clementine laughed. "Gee, thanks."

"Oh, Clementine." Ben's father placed his hand on her back, between her shoulder blades. "Look."

She followed the nod of his head until she saw the vague outline of a musher, off in the distance. He had to be at least a half mile away, but the sight of him sent her reeling. A cloud of snow surrounded him, kicked up by the swift feet of his dog team. As he drew closer, his dogs began to bark, spurred on by the excited cheers of the crowd.

Watching his approach, Clementine's heart expanded. She was full of love—love for her family, love for her friends, both old and new, and love for Alaska itself. But most of all, her heart swelled with love for her husband and the God who'd brought them together, love so strong that it made her chest ache.

Ben's father spoke, breaking the silent spell that had come over her at the sight of her husband. "What do those dogs have on their feet?"

"I'm sure they're wearing booties." Clementine squinted and followed his gaze.

He cleared his throat. "Um, since when do they wear pink booties?"

"Oh. My. Goodness." Anya clutched Clementine's arm. "They *are* pink. He did this for you. Did you know about this?"

"No, I didn't." She shook her head. The pink dog booties were a complete and total surprise.

A very sweet one.

So like Ben, Clementine thought.

As adorable as they were, Clementine had little interest in the booties. All she cared about was getting a good glimpse of Ben.

When he drew close enough for her to make out the familiar outline of his face, her cup of hot chocolate slipped through her fingers. Anya or Sue reached down to pick it up—Clementine couldn't be sure which of them came to her aid. She only had eyes for him.

All around her, people began to shout and cheer. Chants of Ben's name filled the air in a two-beat staccato. *Gray-son, Gray-son, Gray-son.* There wasn't a dry eye in Nome. Everyone in the state was aware of Ben's history. And for the visitors, the newspapers and television stations had all provided detailed coverage of the "musher who'd triumphed over tragedy."

Clementine was barely cognizant of any of it. She held her breath, waiting for the moment when Ben spotted her. The second he did, he blew her a kiss. And in that instant, she forgot he was a world-class dog musher or that he'd at long last conquered his past. He was simply her husband. She blew him a return kiss. Her fingers trembled when she sent it out to him, a reaction that had nothing to do with the cold.

He was so close. Clementine's feet tapped in her bunny boots, itching to break into a run toward Ben's sled. It was all she could do to stand there and wait for his name to be announced over the loudspeaker. When he was less than thirty feet away, he slowed his team to a stop. Race protocol dictated he pause and allow handlers to guide his dogs to the finish, while an official broadcast was made announcing his background and placement.

Clementine watched as a handful of sled dog handlers moved forward to grab hold of the gang line, just as she'd done the year before for Reggie's team. She'd wanted to do the same at the finish for Ben's team this time around, but they'd agreed the dogs would probably be so excited to see Clementine they might ignore Ben's commands and flop down for her to scratch their bellies. Now she was glad she didn't have the responsibility of guiding the dogs through the finish chute. She'd been in no way prepared for the strong emotions this experience would elicit.

Anya and Sue each reached for one of her hands and squeezed them tight while she waited. Ben's father ran forward, past the bright orange fencing and took hold of the line right behind the lead dogs, Kodiak and Moose.

His voice rang out, above all the others, and he waved back at Ben. "I'm proud of you, son."

Ben lifted a hand to his mouth and shook his head, clearly too overcome with emotion to speak.

The announcer's crisp voice boomed over the loudspeaker. "And in sixth place, we have bib number twenty four: Ben Grayson, from Aurora, Alaska. This is Ben's return to the Gold Rush Trail after a five-year absence from competitive dog mushing. Ben's team is comprised solely of rescue dogs. He hails from a long line of mushers, and guess what, folks? He's a newlywed. So maybe one day we'll see the Grayson family tradition continue."

A renewed cheer rose up from the throng of people packed around the finish line and Clementine's cheeks burned. She glanced questioningly at Ben and he just grinned from ear to ear.

"Come on, everyone, let's hear it for Ben Grayson. Bring 'em on in, Ben."

Somehow the dogs heard Ben's Hike command over the rowdy onlookers. With the help of the handlers, they trotted straight into the chute and slowed to an easy stop just past the finish line.

Clementine wasn't sure whether the whoosh she heard when Ben's sled glided past her was the sound of his sled runners or her own gasp of delight. The moment he passed the red line beneath the burled arch, Ben hopped off the sled and headed straight toward her. He peeled off the outermost layers of his extreme cold weather gear as he approached, leaving a trail of beaver-hide mittens and thermal neck gaitors in his wake. The smile on his exhausted face reached all the way to his eyes.

When he reached her, she threw her arms around his neck. Despite the fatigue she knew he must be battling, he lifted her clear off her feet and spun her around. His journey had been long. Far longer than the thousand miles he'd mushed from Aurora to Nome.

"Let me look at you," he breathed.

The world around them ceased to exist. Clementine had no idea where the dogs were. And for once, she didn't care.

He set her down, pushed back the hood of her coat and buried his hands in her curls. "You've no idea how badly I missed you."

"I think I have an inkling." She ran her fingertips over his face, reddened from the sun and wind, and slid the pad of her thumb across his chapped lips. "But you did it, Ben. I'm so happy for you."

"No." He shook his head and his eyes, still as blue as a glacier, grew shiny. "We did it."

Clementine bit her lip to keep herself from falling completely to pieces. She nodded toward the dog team, which Ben's dad seemed to have under control. "Nice booties, by the way."

"You like those?"

"I do." Her bottom lip quivered.

He stilled it with a touch from his fingertip. "I thought you might."

Then he gathered her in his arms and covered her with tender kisses—her hair, her cheeks, her lips—

before whispering in her ear, "He has repaid me for the years the locusts have eaten. And it started the day I met you."

* * * * *

If you enjoyed Teri Wilson's book, be sure to check out the other books this month from Love Inspired!

Dear Reader,

Thank you for reading *Alaskan Hearts*. This story is very near and dear to my heart as it is my first book for Harlequin and the fulfillment of a lifelong dream.

When I made my first trip to Alaska in 2009 to volunteer as a sled dog handler at the famed Iditarod Trail Sled Dog Race, I fell in love with the beauty and spirit of our forty-ninth state. Like Clementine, I was nervous and imagined myself falling down and being trampled by a team of happy, eager Alaskan huskies. Or worse, a sled. But God had planted a dream in my heart and it was up to me to trust Him to see it through. How many times in life are we presented with fantastic opportunities only to pass them by because we are afraid? I didn't fall down that day in Alaska. But if I had, He would have been there to pick me up. God is faithful. We can trust Him with all our dreams and hopes for the future. This is the truth Ben and Clementine both grapple with in these pages.

I went back to Alaska the following year and will continue to do so as long as I'm able. It is a place like no other—wild, rugged and so beautiful it takes my breath away. My prayer is that God will continue to provide me with exciting, new experiences and many more stories to share with you.

Wishing you all of God's blessings and peace,
Teri Wilson

Questions for Discussion

1. Have you ever traveled to a faraway place by yourself? How do you think traveling alone differs from doing so with a companion? Why do you think Clementine brings Nugget with her to Alaska?

2. Why is Clementine so determined not to let Ben tell her what to do? Is her reaction a fair response? Why or why not?

3. When Ben first meets Clementine, he is overcome with the urge to protect her from the dangers of Alaska. Why do you think he feels this way?

4. This story centers around a dog sled race. Before reading it, did you know much about dog mushing? In what ways did the story surprise you about the sport?

5. Clementine is shocked to discover that Ben is a dog musher. Why is she so surprised? And why does she find herself even more drawn to him after this revelation?

6. What do you think of Ben's decision to quit mushing after his accident? Do you think the reaction of his friends and family to this decision was helpful or hurtful?

7. What does Clementine like about her life back home in Texas and in what way does she want her life to change?

8. Have you ever felt the desire to start over again in an entirely new place? In what ways can this be a good idea and in what ways is it not?

9. Ben was close to God before his accident but pulled away afterward. Why do you think some Christians struggle with trusting God after a tragedy more than others?

10. Was the portrayal of Alaska in this story as you expected? Do you feel the Alaskan setting enhanced the romance between Ben and Clementine? Why or why not?

11. What role do the dogs play in this story? Have you ever had a close relationship with a pet before?

12. What sort of memories does Ben struggle with when Clementine asks him to adopt the stray dog she finds?

13. What sort of unique challenges do you imagine Clementine will face once she moves to Alaska? How do you think living there differs from living in other parts of the country?

14. What significance do the Northern Lights play in *Alaskan Hearts?* What does their appearance in Nome symbolize to Ben?

15. What are the central struggles that Ben and Clementine deal with in this book? In what ways do you identify with these characters?

LARGER-PRINT BOOKS!

**GET 2 FREE
LARGER-PRINT NOVELS
PLUS 2 FREE
MYSTERY GIFTS**

Love Inspired

Larger-print novels are now available...